"I'm going to crush you, Lockhart."

"You're welcome to try," Steve replied with a sexy grin. "Who knows? I might even enjoy—" His voice died when he opened the door and realized there was something in the cockpit of his plane.

Casey flushed. "If you think... What's that?"

"It looks like...a baby," Steve answered lamely, studying the tiny sleeping occupant of the molded plastic infant carrier resting on his seat.

Casey gasped. "Oh my God, Steve. It's a baby!"

"That's what I said."

"But whose is it? How did it get here?"

Steve looked quickly around the hangar, but he and Casey were alone—a situation he would have delighted in under different circumstances. "I don't know." He shook his head. "It's too hot to leave the baby out here. We better get it inside."

As he tentatively lifted the carrier out of the plane's cockpit, something fluttered to the ground. Casey bent to pick it up, then showed it to Steve.

He groaned. The note read "Please take care of Annie."

Dear Reader,

One of the most common questions readers ask me is, "Where do you get your ideas?" Well, in this case, I can't take all the credit. The inspiration for this particular story came from my own eldest "baby," Courtney. I was struggling to come up with a story line that fit the BACHELORS & BABIES concept, when Courtney took pity on me. She said, "What if your hero finds a baby on an airplane?" and *The Littlest Stowaway* evolved from that suggestion. She even contributed to the title!

Even though Courtney is a student at the University of Arkansas with the goal of attending medical school, she will always be my "baby"—and one of my most loyal fans. My husband and I consider Courtney, as well as our other extraordinary children, sixteen-year-old Kerry and ten-year-old David, our greatest blessings. The joy my kids have brought me is a large part of the reason children so often appear in the stories I write.

I hope that some of that joy will rub off as you read about a very *little* girl named Annie....

Gina Wilkins

P.S. It looks like the South is rising again.... Don't miss the secrets, the scandals and the seductions when I revisit the SOUTHERN SCANDALS miniseries—and those wild McBrides—next year....

Gina Wilkins
THE LITTLEST STOWAWAY

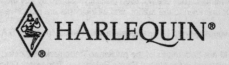

HARLEQUIN®

TORONTO • NEW YORK • LONDON
AMSTERDAM • PARIS • SYDNEY • HAMBURG
STOCKHOLM • ATHENS • TOKYO • MILAN • MADRID
PRAGUE • WARSAW • BUDAPEST • AUCKLAND

For Courtney and John,
who are always willing to brainstorm.
Love you both.

ISBN 0-373-25849-6

THE LITTLEST STOWAWAY

1

"LOCKHART! I WANT to talk to you."

Steven Lockhart grimaced, but didn't slow down as he strode through the parking lot from his car toward his office. Maybe if he pretended he didn't hear her, she would go away.

No such luck. "Darn it, Lockhart, don't ignore me," she called after him. "I have some things to say to you."

He was aware that they had attracted attention—and amusement—from others headed toward their cars after work on this late afternoon in September. The standing feud between Casey Jansen and him was well-known—and widely appreciated—at the small, regional Arkansas airport in which their respective businesses were located. Usually, Steve enjoyed the sparring, if for no other reason than it gave him an excuse to spend time with Casey. But today, he was really in a hurry. No time for fun.

He ducked into the lobby of Lockhart Air and hurried toward his private office. "Tell her I'm not here," he told his impossible-to-ruffle assistant as he rushed past her into his inner sanctum, locking the door behind him. Even as he picked up the phone on his desk and dialed the number of his newest and potentially-most-lucrative customer, he could hear Casey's raised voice through the door.

"What do you mean, he's not here? I *saw* him come in..."

Steve was grinning when he turned his full attention to business.

Half an hour later, he poked his head cautiously out of his office. "Is she gone?"

Madelyn, his office manager and personal assistant, looked up from her work with her usual serene smile. "She's gone. Someone paged her and she stormed out. But I suspect she'll be back."

Of course she will. Steve would be seriously disappointed if she didn't return. In fact, then he would have to find an excuse to go looking for her. The fierce business rivalry between them hadn't stopped Steve from falling head over heels for Casey Jansen, or from making plans to do something about it as soon as the time was right. But he'd like to avoid her until he had time to really enjoy the encounter.

Putting his fiery competitor out of his mind, he stepped through the doorway to lean comfortably against Madelyn's desk. "Any calls while I was out?"

Brushing her straight hair away from her broad, pleasant face, his office manager handed him a stack of yellow message slips. "Nothing you can't handle tomorrow."

"Good. I'm flying to Memphis this evening to talk

to a guy about a used Beechcraft he's got for sale. If I can get him to come down a few thousand, we might just have ourselves another plane for our fleet." He said the last word a bit ironically, since Lockhart Air's "fleet" consisted of only three planes.

Madelyn nodded. "Sounds good. Don't bankrupt us."

Steve chuckled, accepting her pragmatic warning the way she'd intended. He knew how precarious their financial situation was. New businesses often failed in the first year or two of operation, and Steve was still treading that dangerous line with his fledgling air charter service. Single, thirty-five-year-old Madelyn kept the books for his company, and she guarded the money as if it were her own. Steve liked it that way, being somewhat bookkeeping-challenged, himself.

Madelyn was short and broad and no-nonsense, intimidating to some people, but she had the kindest heart and most even disposition of anyone Steve knew. He had begun to think of her almost as a sister during the two years they'd worked together, and he respected her competence, her intelligence, and her deeply-buried dry humor.

"Has B.J. checked in yet?" he asked her.

Madelyn wrinkled her nose. "No. He's giving a lesson to Mrs. Hood."

Steve groaned sympathetically. Avis Hood had been taking flying lessons for almost a year now and was still the scariest student pilot in all of central Arkansas. B.J. had the patience of a saint to keep working with her, even though others might have already tried to convince her she should keep her dainty feet firmly planted on solid ground. Fortunately, she enjoyed the lessons and was willing to pay well for the service, so Steve hoped B.J.'s patience didn't run out too soon. Avis's cash would come in handy if they bought that fourth plane.

An overflowing wastebasket beside Madelyn's desk caught his eye. "Still no word from Janice?"

His office manager's usually serene face creased with a frown. "Nothing. I'm very worried about her."

Steve shared her concern. "I'm worried, too," he admitted. "But I don't know what else to do."

The young woman who had cleaned their offices every afternoon for the past six months hadn't been seen since Friday evening. Janice was in her early twenties, single, and claimed to have no family. She was also at least eight months pregnant.

When Janice hadn't shown up Monday, they had tried calling her, but there'd been no answer at the only number she'd provided them. Since she had always been completely reliable, calling if she was running even a few minutes later than usual, Steve had been worried enough by Tuesday to drive to the tiny, run-down trailer park in which Janice lived.

There'd been no answer when he'd knocked on her door, and he'd looked in every window, finding no sign of anyone in the dilapidated mobile home.

The trailer park manager had informed him that Janice's rent was paid through the end of the month, but he hadn't seen her lately. Not that he saw her often, he'd added, remarking that Janice spent a lot of time alone in her trailer, never received visitors and always paid her rent on time. He wished all his tenants were so little trouble, he'd added, lazily scratching his sagging belly.

And now it was Friday again, and there hadn't been a word from Janice. Madelyn had been doing the basic cleaning, but Steve was worried about more than the dust collecting on the furniture.

"I should have insisted she give us an emergency number," Steve grumbled. "Surely there's *someone* who knows or cares where she is."

Before Madelyn could reply, a familiar voice spoke from the doorway. "*There* you are. Don't even try to run away from me this time, Lockhart."

His mouth quirking into a wry smile, Steve turned to face Casey Jansen. As always, the sight of her filled him with both pleasure and bemusement. She was dressed professionally, as usual, looking as if she'd just stepped out of a meeting in her blue sheath dress with sensible navy pumps. There was no question that she was a striking woman, her heart-shaped face framed by light brown hair that fell to the middle of her back, her eyes a dark, smoky blue, her mouth full and soft.

Steve had developed a near obsession with that pouty mouth of hers; he was growing increasingly impatient to find out exactly how it tasted. Even though she would probably knock him senseless if he tried. He was well aware that she wasn't ready to even acknowledge the simmering attraction he'd sensed between them from the first time they'd met—much less to do anything about it.

He wasn't exactly her favorite person, but at least he suspected she thought of him often. Just as he thought of her during most of his waking moments—and all too many of his sleeping ones too, lately. She'd played a prominent part in more than a few recent uncomfortable dreams.

Though he knew what she wanted to talk to him about, he sidetracked her with a question of his own. "I don't suppose you've heard from Janice?"

Casey blinked. "Janice?"

"You know, the woman who cleans your offices every evening, right after she does mine?"

"Yes, I know who she is. I think it's obvious that she quit."

He lifted an eyebrow. "She gave you notice?"

"No, but neither did the last one."

"The last one got busted for growing the wrong kind of 'herbs' in her kitchen garden," Steve reminded Casey dryly. "Madelyn and I are worried that Janice is in trouble. She's been acting very nervous lately, and it isn't like her not to call. No one has seen her at her trailer all week."

"She must have gone back to her family. Or her baby's father," Casey suggested. "I wondered how much longer she would be able to work. I asked her last week if her doctor approved of her doing manual labor so late in her pregnancy, but she said he told her she could work as long as it was comfortable for her." She shrugged. "I guess it stopped being comfortable."

Steve frowned at her. He knew Casey's management techniques were different from his own—he was a people person, she was into bottom-line numbers—but he'd never believed her to be truly cold. "You're not at all concerned about her?"

Her expression changed, letting him see the genuine worry she'd been trying to hide behind her brusque words. "I've been concerned about her since I found out she was twenty-two, alone, unmarried and pregnant," she admitted. "But every time I asked if I could help her, she made it very clear it was none of my business. I would say she has sent the same message to all of us by quitting without a call. As much as I hated to do it, I've instructed my secretary to call a janitorial service to clean our offices this weekend, and then we're going to hire someone new to start next week. I suggest you do the same."

"Janice wouldn't just quit without calling," Madelyn said stubbornly. "She'll be back when she can."

"Yet our trash cans are filling up and our bathrooms need scrubbing. We can't just put everything on hold until she decides to return," Casey retorted, running a slender hand through her hair in a gesture that struck Steve as rather weary. He'd often accused her of working too hard to keep the business she had recently inherited more successful than his. His concern for her hadn't softened her, of course; she'd implied that he wanted her to slow down so he could make even more headway in their professional competition.

She didn't give him an inch. Casey was fiery, stubborn, prickly and a bit paranoid when it came to him. And he was certifiably crazy about her. When the time was right, he reminded himself, he would try to convince her of that.

In the meantime, he thought with a glance at his watch, he had business to attend to. "I've got to be on my way. Madelyn, go home. It's nearly six. You've put in enough hours today. I'll see you Monday. If you hear from Janice, tell her I'll help her any way I can. Casey, it was a pleasure to see you, as always."

Her eyes widened. "Now, wait a minute. We aren't through. I need to talk to you about...damn it, Lockhart, don't you dare walk away from me again."

He was already halfway out the side door on his way to the plane he'd left prepped. "Sorry, darlin', but I've got an appointment. Maybe we can talk next week."

She was on his heels as he stepped into the slowly cooling early-evening air. The heat from the day had built up in the asphalt and now radiated upward through the soles of the boots he wore with his jeans and cotton shirt. He was glad he'd left the plane in the fan-cooled hangar rather than out on the tarmac, where the cockpit would be as hot as Hades by now.

A hand clutched his arm. "I hate it when you ignore me this way," Casey complained.

He grinned and patted her hand with his. "I know you do, Casey, darlin'. But you've got to admit it gives you a great excuse to chase after me."

She jerked her hand from his, her eyes flashing blue fire. "In your dreams."

"Frequently," he agreed, thinking of one particular dream involving the two of them and a tropical island...

She eyed him uncertainly, looking disconcerted as she always did when he hinted at his attraction to her. He wanted to think she even looked a bit tempted to return his flirting occasionally—not that she had ever allowed herself to do so. Yet.

And then she shook her head, obviously assuming he was merely taunting her again. "I want to know what you did to steal George McNalley from me," she snapped, getting to the subject he'd known was on her mind. "He's been a satisfied JCS customer for five years. And now I find that he's suddenly working with you, instead. What did you tell him? What promises did you make him?"

Moving into the hangar with Casey right behind him, Steve put a hand on his airplane, lovingly caressing the gleaming white wing. He couldn't help looking forward to a peaceful, solitary flight. "I promised him dependable, reliable service at an excellent price."

"*I've* been giving him that," she protested.

"Face it, Casey. I underbid you. And besides," he added a bit smugly, "he likes me."

She made a sound that was somewhere between a growl and an oath. "You pulled your good-ol'-boy routine on him, didn't you? Did you make him believe a man is more qualified to run a charter service than a woman? He's one of the customers who worried that I wouldn't be able to keep the business running after my father died, isn't he? Did you play on that archaic sexism?"

Steve moved his hand to the door handle of his plane. "Casey, I think you are entirely qualified to run Jansen Charter Service. You've been doing so quite efficiently for a year now. You're a damned tough competitor—but so am I. As far as business is concerned, you being a woman makes no difference to me at all. I won't underestimate you because of it, and I won't give you any breaks because of it. I'm going to keep offering outstanding service at bargain prices and if that cuts into your business—well, that's life."

After a momentary pause, she muttered, "I'm going to crush you, Lockhart."

"You're welcome to try," he replied equably. "Just as you've been trying for the past year. But I have no more intention of being crushed now than I did when you started. Now, if you'll excuse me, I have to..."

His voice died when he opened the door and realized there was someone sitting in the pilot's seat of his plane.

"If you think I... What's that?" Casey's attention, like his, had been abruptly captured.

"It looks like...a baby," Steve said lamely, studying the tiny, sleeping occupant of the molded plastic infant carrier resting on his seat. A baby that was so small, so still, he wondered for a moment if it was a doll.

And then it moved, its little mouth puckering in apparent discontent.

Casey gasped. "Oh, my God, Steve. It's a baby!"

He sent her an exasperated look. "That's what I said."

"Whose is it? How did it get here?"

He looked quickly around the hangar, but he and Casey were alone. Even Ralph, his mechanic, had left for the day. Whoever had left the baby in the plane had to have done so within the past half hour to avoid being seen. "I don't know."

The infant moved restlessly in the carrier, its miniscule fingers opening and closing. In deference to the heat, it was dressed only in a thin white cotton shirt and a diaper beneath the snugly buckled straps of the infant carrier.

Casey continued to stare into the cockpit. "Steve, this baby can't be more than a few days old."

"I...uh..." Shock seemed to have affected his ability to speak clearly; all he could manage was a stammer.

"You weren't *expecting* to find a baby here, were you?" she prodded. "Is this why you were in such a hurry?"

He stared at her. "No, I wasn't expecting to find a baby in my plane. What kind of a question is that?"

"You mean someone just left it here? You don't think—you don't think it has been abandoned, do you?"

"Who would abandon a baby in my plane?" he repeated, shaking his head in disbelief. If this was a practical joke, it was a sick one, he thought, looking around one more time in the hope of seeing someone who would claim the child and explain its presence there. But the hangar was still empty except for Casey and himself—and the baby in his airplane.

"We should take it inside," Casey said, her voice a bit uncertain. "It's too hot out here."

"Inside?" he parroted blankly.

"In your office. It's closer than mine. We can call the police from there."

"The police?"

Casey rolled her eyes. "Will you stop repeating me? Of course, we must call the police. That's what you're supposed to do when you find an abandoned baby. For all we know, the baby needs immediate medical attention—and it looks like it's up to us to make sure it gets help."

Steve looked at the baby again, wondering why the thought of turning it over to the police bothered him so badly. But he supposed Casey was right. If someone really had dumped the child here—for reasons he simply could not comprehend—they had no choice but to notify the proper authorities. "Okay. You carry it."

"Me?" She hastily put her hands behind her back. "No, I'd better not. I might drop it. You carry it."

He frowned at her. All of a sudden Miss I-Can-Do-Anything-You-Can-Do was going to play helpless? Seeing no alternative, he tentatively lifted the infant carrier, which hadn't been buckled into the seat. It was surprisingly light, he thought, balancing it by the molded carrying handle. The baby must not weigh more than six or seven pounds.

Something fluttered to the ground when he lifted the carrier out of the plane. Casey bent to retrieve it.

"What does it say?" Steve asked, studying her face as she read the words printed on the slip of paper.

Her voice wasn't quite steady when she read the few stark words. "'Please take care of Annie.'" Casey looked up at him then with a thunderstruck expression. "That's all it says. No signature."

Please take care of Annie. The simple request struck Steve sharply as he looked down at the flushed face of the tiny, helpless infant. "You must be Annie," he murmured.

The child's only reaction was to stir restlessly in her seat.

He looked up to find Casey gazing somberly at him. "Someone abandoned this baby," she said, as if the reality of it was just beginning to sink in.

Steve swallowed. "Let's get her inside."

Maybe he could think more clearly once they were in his office. But he still didn't think he'd have a clue what he was going to do with a newborn baby.

CASEY BIT HER LIP as she followed Steve back into his office. He walked more slowly now than he had when she'd tried to catch him earlier, she noted. He carried the baby as carefully as if it were made of spun glass. Even in the plastic carrier, the baby looked impossibly tiny in Steve's strong arms.

She was still finding it hard to believe that someone had left an infant in Steve Lockhart's plane. It made no sense to her at all. It was such a warm day. So much could have gone wrong. What if Steve hadn't been going up in that particular plane? What if he'd locked the hangar without looking inside? Had the mother been watching from some hidden vantage point to make sure her baby would be safe? Pausing for a moment outside Steve's office, she looked around, but no one seemed to be paying any particular attention to them. For all she knew, whoever had left the baby in Steve's plane could be in another state by now.

Despite Steve's parting instructions, Madelyn was still at her desk. She was chatting with a mountain of a man whose bushy red hair and beard clashed cheerfully with his shocking-pink shirt. Ragged jeans and green high-topped sneakers completed his ensemble. Casey shook her head in silent disapproval, as she always did when she saw B. J. Smith, who worked as a pilot and flight instructor for Lockhart Air. Her own pilots wore crisply pressed khaki shirts embroidered with the Jansen Charter Service logo. Professional appearances were important to her, as they had been to her father.

And still she was losing longtime customers to Lockhart, she thought with a frisson of panic. Steve was steadily cutting into the narrow profit she'd been able to manage after her father's long-undiagnosed illness had caused him to make disastrous decisions that had almost been the ruin of JCS. She vowed that George McNalley would be the last customer she would lose to Steve Lockhart. She was determined to prove that her father—as well as several others—had been wrong when they had predicted that she would lose the business her grandfather had founded so many years ago.

Her attention was reclaimed by a deep bellow. "Hey, Steve, we thought you were—what the hell is that?" B.J.'s green eyes widened as he stared at the infant carrier in his employer's hands.

"It's a baby," Madelyn pronounced, just a hint of puzzlement in her matter-of-fact voice.

"Madelyn wins this round," Steve commented, carefully setting the carrier on her desk.

"So...you and Casey've been busy, huh?" B.J. asked with a broad grin that made Casey scowl.

"This is not funny, B.J.," she said repressively. "Someone abandoned this poor baby in Steve's plane."

That wiped the grin from the irreverent pilot's face. "*Abandoned?*" he repeated. "Are you kidding?"

His brown eyes dark with concern, Steve shook his head. "When I opened the door, there it was. No one else was in the hangar."

"We found this note," Casey added, displaying the slip of paper so that B.J. and Madelyn could read the few words printed on it.

"Whoa." B.J. rubbed the back of his neck and looked uncharacteristically solemn as he eyed the restlessly dozing baby. "What are you going to do?"

"We're going to call the police, of course," Casey answered when Steve hesitated. "They'll send someone to investigate and take custody of the baby."

"No." Madelyn's quick interjection brought everyone's attention to her.

"What do you mean, no?" Casey frowned. "Of course we have to call the police. Abandoning a baby is a crime. And this child needs immediate attention. We don't know how long it has been since she was fed, or how long she was in that plane."

Casey was suddenly worried that the baby's sleep wasn't natural. Shouldn't the noise and movement have roused her by now? She and Steve had been stunned into near-immobility by finding the baby, but now it was time for someone to take action. Since everyone still seemed almost paralyzed by shock, it looked as though it was up to her. She reached for the phone on Madelyn's desk.

Madelyn's hand covered hers on the receiver. "Wait."

"Madelyn, we really can't wait any longer."

As if she'd finally realized that something momentous was going on around her, the baby chose that moment to awaken with a startled cry. Her blue eyes opened wide and unfocused, and her tiny hands and feet pumped the air. She began to cry in high, thin wails, surprisingly loud for such miniscule lungs.

Steve tried rocking the carrier, speaking in soothing, nonsensical syllables that had no effect.

"You should probably pick her up," B.J. offered. "My sister's babies usually stopped crying when someone held them."

"Uh...Madelyn?" Steve asked hopefully.

Madelyn shook her head. "She's too tiny. I'd be too nervous."

Steve turned to Casey. "I don't suppose you..."

"You try holding her," she said quickly, terrified at the very thought of lifting that squirming, squalling infant out of the baby carrier. "She's probably hungry. I'll make the call."

She tried again to lift the receiver, but again Madelyn stopped her. "Don't."

After drawing a deep breath, Steve unbuckled the safety straps of the carrier and awkwardly slid his big hands beneath the baby's head and hips. He lifted her carefully into his arms, cradling her against his broad chest. Watching him, Casey realized her throat had tightened, for some reason. There was just something about watching a big, strong man holding a tiny, helpless infant—especially a man as ruggedly handsome and potently sexy as Steve Lockhart, qualities she'd been reluctantly aware of for longer than she wanted to admit.

She quickly turned her attention to Madelyn, raising her voice a bit to be heard over the baby's cries. "Why don't you want me to call the police? Surely you know it's the only thing we can do."

But again, Madelyn shook her head. "What if it's Janice's baby?" she asked simply. "What if she's brought her to us because she needs our help?"

2

MADELYN'S QUESTION made Casey go still. She hadn't even considered the possibility that this was Janice's baby. She glanced at Steve, who was still futilely rocking the unhappy infant. He didn't look particularly surprised by the possibility, she realized. Had it already occurred to him?

"Janice's baby isn't even due for another couple of weeks, is it?" she asked hesitantly.

"The baby's not very big," B.J. mused. "What would you say it weighs, Steve? Six pounds?"

"Maybe," Steve conceded, studying the little body in his arms. "No more than that."

"So it could have been a week or so early," B.J. concluded. "And it doesn't look more than a few days old. No one has seen Janice for—what?—a week? I guess it could be hers."

Casey's head was starting to hurt. "Why would Janice have left her baby in Steve's plane? That's just crazy."

"I told you she's in trouble," Madelyn murmured.

"If Janice is the mother, then she left the baby with us for a reason," Steve said, motioning toward the note on the desk. "She thought we would help her."

B.J. nodded somberly. "She must be desperate."

Casey looked at all of them in open disbelief. "You really think Janice left her newborn baby in Steve's plane?"

"You have to admit it's possible," Steve said.

Considering everything, it *was* possible, Casey thought. "Maybe," she said grudgingly. "But that doesn't change the fact that we have to contact the authorities."

B.J. frowned. "You'd call the cops on Janice?" he asked, his tone accusatory.

She immediately went on the defensive. Couldn't these people see that she was worried about the baby—and now about Janice, as well? "B.J., if the baby is Janice's, she's obviously in trouble. She needs help."

"The police won't help her," Madelyn murmured. "They'll arrest her for endangering the welfare of a minor. And then they'll take her baby away from her."

"What makes you think she wants the baby?"

"Because she asked Steve to take care of her. She'll be back when she can."

Casey shook her head. "You can't know that."

"I know that if she'd wanted to give the baby away, she wouldn't have left her with Steve."

"Madelyn, if she'd only wanted a baby-sitter, this is hardly the way she'd have gone about it."

"I'm going to look around the hangar," B.J. announced abruptly, moving toward the door. "Maybe

I'll find something that will give us an idea of what's going on here."

Casey put her hands on her hips, looking from Madelyn's stubborn face to Steve's harried one as he rhythmically jiggled the still-fussing baby. "Steve? Surely you agree we have to report this."

He grimaced ruefully. "I don't know, Casey. If this *is* Janice's baby, it seems she's asking for our help."

Had they all lost their minds? "Steve, this is a baby, not a puppy she's asked you to watch while she's on vacation for a few days. Are you actually considering taking this child home with you? How are you going to take care of it? How long are you going to wait before calling the authorities—until the kid starts school?"

He sighed. "I don't know," he admitted. "I just don't feel right about calling the police now."

Casey threw up her hands in exasperation. "I can't believe you're even hesitating. Have you considered the possibility that you'd be breaking the law by not reporting this? Do you want to go to jail?"

"It's not against the law to baby-sit for a friend," he said defensively.

She was getting very close to grinding her teeth. "This isn't baby-sitting. This is abandonment. *Reckless* abandonment. Do you know how many things could have gone wrong before you just happened to find the baby in your plane?"

"You really think we should call the police?" he asked, turning the question back to her. "You think we should give them Janice's name and turn the baby over to child welfare services?"

He made it sound so cold, she thought with resentment. Just because she was the type who believed in following rules, obeying the law, that didn't mean she had no feelings. She could only imagine the desperation that would compel a woman to abandon a newborn, but she couldn't condone the action, or allow it to go unreported. Someone had to be rational and responsible here. As was so often the case, she was the logical candidate. "I can't see that we have any other option."

Madelyn frowned in disapproval.

Steve hesitated a moment, then caught Casey completely off guard by suddenly depositing the baby in her arms. Her arms tightened reflexively, automatically cradling the baby's head.

"Okay," he said. "*You* turn her in. I don't think I can do it."

Oh, this wasn't fair. Aware that Steve and Madelyn were watching her closely, Casey glanced down at the fretting baby, who gazed tearfully, blearily back up at her. For some reason, Annie suddenly stopped crying and snuggled more securely into Casey's arms, as though in search of security and reassurance. And Casey melted.

She'd never held a baby this tiny before. She had never realized quite how good it would feel. Or how simply holding such a helpless little one would bring out protective, undeniably maternal instincts Casey had never even known she possessed.

She tried to remind herself that she had the baby's best interest at heart by calling in the authorities. There were people trained to deal with situations like this—and no one in this room fit that description. Annie needed to be with people who knew how to take care of her.

"Janice cleans your bathrooms," Madelyn murmured as if that argument should carry some weight in Casey's decision.

The baby whimpered and clutched at Casey's clothes with her tiny, unsteady fingers. Casey's heart lodged firmly in her throat.

"Give me the weekend to find Janice," Steve said, watching her as if sensing her sudden weakening. "If we haven't heard from her by Monday, we'll call the authorities."

"We could all be in big trouble for not reporting this immediately," Casey was compelled to warn them, even though she had to force her voice past the lump in her throat.

"I'm willing to take that chance if it will help Janice," Steve answered steadily.

"So am I," Madelyn agreed.

"Count me in." B.J. entered the office carrying a brown paper bag. "I found this in the plane. It's full of baby bottles and disposable diapers, but there was nothing else useful and no sign of Janice."

"Casey? She didn't have anyone else to turn to," Steve reminded her. "She's trusting us to help her."

Casey didn't bother to point out that technically *she* hadn't been included. Janice would have had no way of knowing that Casey would be with Steve when he found the baby. Janice had rebuffed her offers to help her before. Maybe she would have suspected that Casey's first impulse would be to call the authorities, whereas Steve and his associates would be more likely to follow their hearts?

She bit her lip. It wasn't easy for her to break the rules. She wasn't the type who took reckless risks or played life by ear. Her well-honed common sense was reminding her impatiently that she knew what she was supposed to do in a situation like this, and she should be doing it. But she kept picturing Janice as she'd last seen her—young, pregnant. Alone.

Annie stirred again in Casey's arms, making funny, kittenish sounds that almost sounded like pleas. Casey sighed, surrendering for once to her heart. "Okay," she said, speaking primarily to Steve. "We'll probably all go to jail, but I won't call anyone at the moment. We'll give Janice a chance to come to her senses first. But if we haven't heard from her by Monday, we'll have to notify the police."

He nodded, his eyes gleaming with approval at her decision. The way he looked at her made her swallow hard. She had never really known how to take his incessant flirting and teasing. She'd never known whether he really was attracted to her, or simply enjoyed mocking her even as he tried to put her out of business. Even if the attraction was real, she couldn't allow herself to trust him, she reminded herself. Her very livelihood, as well as that of her employees, depended on her keeping a cool head when she was around this dangerously charming male.

"We'll give it until Monday," he agreed.

Casey gulped, wondering what on earth she'd just gotten herself into.

EVERYONE AGREED that "li'l orphan Annie," as B.J. had nicknamed the baby, was hungry. She made that clear enough with her lusty wails and frantic fist-suckling. Unfortunately none of the adults in the room had any experience with babies. The paper bag B.J. had discovered in the plane held several plastic bottles, a can of powdered infant formula, and perhaps a dozen tiny disposable diapers.

Steve eyed the can of formula doubtfully. The dry powder didn't look particularly satisfying—or appetizing—to him. "This is all the kid needs to eat?"

Casey transferred the baby to his arms, taking the can of formula from him without meeting his eyes. "All we have to do is read the directions," she said, returning now to her usual efficient manner. "We need sterile water," she added, glancing at the label.

"There's bottled water in the kitchen," Madelyn volunteered. "And a microwave."

Casey nodded. "I'll prepare a bottle. Someone

should probably check the baby's diaper while I'm gone."

Steve looked at B.J., who held up his huge, rough hands and shook his shaggy head. "Don't look at me. As big as I am, I'm scared to even touch that little bitty girl."

Both men looked at Madelyn. "I've never changed a diaper," she said with a shrug. "Only child, remember? Never even had a baby-sitting job while I was growing up."

Steve made a face. "I haven't changed a diaper since I was twelve and my kid brother was a toddler."

"Looks like you're elected," B.J. said in relief. "You've had experience, however far in the past."

Steve seized on the only excuse that occurred to him. "But she's a girl."

Madelyn's eyes glinted with sudden humor. "B.J. and I will chaperone."

He swallowed, knowing when he was defeated. "Clear a spot on your desk, will you?"

Madelyn had already cleaned her desk for the day, leaving the wooden surface uncluttered except for her open week-at-a-glance calendar and a plastic container full of sharpened pencils. She moved those aside and laid out a clean diaper. "Change away."

It was a terrifying experience. The baby cried and squirmed, looking so small and fragile that Steve's fingers shook slightly when he touched her. He changed her as quickly as possible, thinking he should probably have baby wipes or powder or something, but making do with a clean, dry diaper.

"There's nothing else for her to wear in that bag?" Madelyn asked, touching a cautious fingertip to the baby's thin white cotton shirt.

Standing at a safe distance from the diapering area, B.J. shook his head. "That's all I found."

"Here's the bottle." Casey reappeared just as Annie wound up to howl again. "I hope I did it right. I warmed it just a little more than room temperature."

"I'm sure it's fine," Steve replied. "Why don't you sit in Madelyn's chair while you feed her?"

"While *I* feed her?"

"Hey, I changed her."

Casey looked at Madelyn, who shook her head, and at B.J., who backed away in alarm. "All right. I'll feed her," she conceded, turning back to Steve with an air of resignation.

She sat in Madelyn's comfortable office chair and Steve laid the baby in her arms. For a moment, it seemed the unhappy infant would reject the rubber nipple Casey tried to offer. The adults held their breaths until the child finally latched on and began to nurse noisily. There was a collective sigh of relief when the crying was finally silenced.

Steve ran a hand through his hair. "I'd better call and cancel my meeting in Memphis. B.J., why don't you stop at Janice's trailer park on your way home, see if anyone has heard from her?"

B.J. nodded. "I'll see what I can find out."

Steve turned to Madelyn. "You might as well go home. Your mother will be worried. If you can think of anyone to call who might know something about Janice..."

"I'll think about it, but I don't know anyone who knows her."

He nodded. "All right. I'll see you Monday."

Madelyn hesitated, looking from him to the baby in Casey's arms. "What are you going to do with the baby?"

"I'll take care of her," he promised rashly. *Somehow.*

He was doing this for Janice, he reminded himself. He only hoped she repaid her faith in him by coming back to claim her baby and then convincing him that she would never do anything like this again.

When B.J. and Madelyn were gone, Steve turned back to Casey, who was watching the baby in obvious fascination. Something about the way she looked at Annie made Steve smile—and fall for her all over again.

He cleared his throat, which had suddenly grown tight, and tried to dilute the awkward intimacy of the moment. "You should probably burp her."

She looked up at him, blinking as though she was surprised to find him still standing there—hardly a boost to his ego. "What?" she asked.

Get ahold of yourself, Lockhart. Concentrate on the baby. "I don't think she should take the whole bottle without burping. It might give her colic—or, uh, or something."

One corner of Casey's mouth twitched with what might have been amusement at his expense. "You don't really know much about babies, do you, Lockhart?"

"No. Do you?"

She made a face. "No."

Carefully, she pulled the nipple away from the baby's mouth and set the bottle on the desk. And then she lifted Annie to her shoulder, awkwardly trying to support her wobbly little head with one hand and pat her back at the same time. It only took a moment for a noisy burp to emerge—along with a mouthful of regurgitated formula that trickled down Casey's arm. "Oh, yuck," she said. "That is so disgusting."

Grimacing sympathetically, Steve moved toward the bathroom. "I'll get a damp paper towel."

"Thanks." Casey stuck the bottle back into the baby's searching mouth.

Since Casey's hands were occupied, Steve wiped her arm for her, efficiently removing all evidence of formula. Just because he liked touching her, he lingered over the task a bit longer than necessary. When she gave him a sudden, narrow-eyed look of warning, he pulled his hand away—noticing that he'd strayed perilously close to the soft curve of her breast—and tossed the paper towel into the wastebasket. Then he remained kneeling at Casey's side, just because it was nice to be so close to her when they weren't fighting, for a change. He reached out to stroke Annie's downy hair with one finger. "She was hungry, wasn't she?"

"Yes." Casey's smoky blue eyes were worried when she met his gaze. "Steve, what are we doing?"

He couldn't resist glancing at her soft, unsmiling mouth which was so temptingly close to his. What *were* they doing? Oh, right. "We're helping a friend."

She captured her lower lip between her teeth. If only she knew the gesture made his own mouth go dry.

"I'm not at all sure we've done the right thing," she fretted. "For all we know, Janice might want us to turn the baby over so a good home can be found for her. We have no way of knowing if she'll come back—or if she'll make a good mother if she does. Leaving Annie this way—I don't know, Steve. It's such an irresponsible thing to do."

"It seems that way, but I'm sure she knew I would help her out. She must have thought she was leaving the baby in good hands. Or at least in friendly hands," he amended ruefully. "I have a feeling she was lurking somewhere around to make sure the baby was safe, even though we didn't see her. There has to be a reason for what she's done, even if we can't imagine what it is right now."

Casey didn't look notably relieved. "And if she doesn't turn up by Monday?"

"I already promised I'll call the authorities," he reminded her. "If there are legal repercussions for the delay—well, I'll deal with them. I don't even have to mention your name, if you want. As far as anyone will know, you never laid eyes on this kid."

"That's very generous of you," Casey responded dryly. "But I'm afraid I am involved. I'm a witness. I can't just pretend I wasn't here."

"So serious and responsible," Steve murmured, smiling as he lifted a hand to brush a strand of hair away from her face. "Do you ever break the rules, Casey, darlin'?"

Her cheeks went pink. "Not very often," she said repressively. "And I've asked you to stop calling me that."

"But I like calling you that." He also liked looking at her, sitting so primly in Madelyn's chair, holding the baby. The sight evoked fantasies he doubted she would appreciate at the moment.

The bottle wasn't quite empty when Annie fell asleep. Casey managed to jostle one more burp out of her—a dry one this time—and then the baby settled down for a sound nap. Steve helped Casey lay Annie in the carrier, snugly fastening the straps. They both stepped back with a sigh of relief.

"Okay, she's changed, fed and sleeping. Now what?" Casey asked, turning to face him.

"Uh—now I guess I take her home."

"You're taking her home?"

"Yeah."

"*Your* home?"

He nodded.

"By yourself?"

"Unless you want to come with us," he suggested hopefully.

She surprised him by hesitating just a moment before she shook her head. "I'm not going home with you."

He smiled ruefully. "Can't blame me for trying."

"Surely you have someone who can help you out. Your, um, girlfriend, maybe?"

"Now, darlin', you know I've been hoping you would fill that vacancy," he chided.

Though her cheeks flamed, she pointedly ignored his remark. "What about your mother?"

"She lives in Dallas."

"Don't try to convince me you don't know any women. I won't believe it."

"Actually, I don't know anyone who'd be interested in helping with a newborn," he admitted. "And besides, the fewer people who know about this for now, the better."

"So you're actually going to try to take care of this baby all weekend by yourself?"

He swallowed and looked at the helpless infant in the plastic carrier. "I can handle it," he said, hoping he sounded more confident than he felt.

"You don't know how to make a bottle."

"I can read directions, same as you did."

A worried frown creased her forehead. "What if

something goes wrong? What if she gets sick or something?"

He wasn't flattered that she was looking at him with such lack of assurance. "I can handle it," he repeated, more firmly this time.

Casey reached out to touch the baby's tiny hand. Annie's fingers curled reflexively. "You don't even have a change of clothing for her."

"As long as I have clean diapers, we'll get by."

Casey still looked worried. "I would give you a hand for a while this evening, but I have an appointment at eight." She glanced at her watch. "As it is, I'm going to have to hurry or I'll be late."

Steve wondered if she had a hot date. The prospect wasn't one that pleased him—even though she would have correctly pointed out that it was none of his business. "Go ahead," he said, knowing his voice had cooled a bit. "Annie and I will be fine."

Shifting her feet, she looked from Steve to the baby and back again. "Do you have a safe place for her to sleep? She's not old enough to move around much, I think, but you have to be sure nothing covers her face. And I don't think she'd be very comfortable staying in this carrier thing all night..."

"Casey, go to your appointment. I said I would take care of Annie, and I will."

She bit her lower lip, then snatched a pencil and a slip of notepaper from Madelyn's desk. "This is my home phone number. If you need my help, call me.

Monday morning, after we've settled this one way or another, burn this number."

He grinned. "I'll have committed it to heart by then."

"Then I'll change it." With one last, worried look at the baby, she moved slowly toward the door. "I hope that carrier is also a safe car seat. Put her in the back, belted in tightly, facing out the back window. Air bags are deadly to infants."

"I've watched the news, Casey. I know about air bags. Now go. We'll be fine."

She was still looking nervously over her shoulder when she left the room.

Steve was left alone with the sleeping baby.

He cleared his throat, ran a hand through his hair, and drew in a deep breath. "Well, Annie, looks like it's just you and me now. God help you."

He glanced at the note still lying on Madelyn's desk. *Please take care of Annie.* "Janice," he murmured, "I hope you know what you're doing."

3

CASEY WAS HAVING trouble concentrating. She tried to pay attention as Edward McClary told her every detail of his day, but her thoughts kept drifting to her own stressful afternoon. She hoped she'd made the right decision when she'd allowed Steve and his employees to talk her out of calling the police.

She wondered how Steve was getting along. Was he taking good care of the baby? Did he know how and when to feed her? Would he know what to do if something went wrong? Annie was so tiny, so fragile. What if something terrible happened? What if she stopped breathing during the night? What if she'd been out in that hot airplane too long that afternoon?

"Casey, are you listening to me?"

Guiltily aware that she hadn't heard a thing her stepbrother had said for the past five minutes or so, Casey looked across the restaurant table at him. "I'm sorry, Edward, I'm afraid I have been a bit distracted this evening. I encountered some...problems at work today."

A quick frown crossed his handsome face. Edward, Casey knew, didn't like her stressing about her work—not because he resented her inattention, but because he had been fretful since she took over JCS that the burden would be too much for her. While she appreciated his concern, Casey found it a bit exasperating. Edward was one of the doubters she felt she had to prove something to by making JCS as strong and profitable as it had been in its heyday under her father's management.

"What's wrong?" he asked quickly. "Is there anything I can do to help?"

She wondered what he would do if she told him exactly what had happened, and the decision she had made not to contact the authorities. He would hit the ceiling, she imagined. He would be convinced that she would be hauled off to jail, or that some dire consequence would result from her uncharacteristic irresponsibility. Edward was a compulsive worrier—and often directed those worries toward his stepsister, for whom he had felt responsible ever since his widowed mother had married Casey's widowed father when Edward was ten and Casey only six.

"Never mind, Edward," she told him with a forced smile. "It isn't anything I can't handle."

"You're sure? Casey, I really wish you would listen to my advice—for once—and consider selling the business. Or at least taking on a partner. I worry about you. You spend too much time and energy on the business, and not enough on your own needs."

She sighed. "I've told you before—repeatedly—

that I am perfectly capable of running JCS and I have no intention of selling. Nor do I need a partner." And then she smiled. "Unless you're applying for the position?"

As she had known he would, Edward practically shuddered. "I'm perfectly content with the job I have, thank you."

A cosmetic dentist, Edward had never been interested in his stepfather's company. He couldn't comprehend why Casey was so determined to put in fourteen-hour days and court ulcers and migraines just to keep Jansen Charter Service in operation. He had also never understood how insulting she found his assumption that, because she was a young woman, she wasn't qualified to run the business.

Despite their differences and the lack of a real blood relationship between them, Casey and Edward had worked to maintain a relationship even after Edward's mother died five years ago and Casey's father's death last year. They dined together once a month and spoke on the phone a time or two in between. The tenuous connection between them was important to both of them—probably because it was the only family bond either of them had left.

Except for Edward and a few distant cousins, Casey was almost as alone as Janice, she realized somberly. Yet, if she found herself abandoned, broke and pregnant, she knew she could turn to her stepbrother. Had Janice truly had no one to help her?

Was that the reason she had put her fate in Steve Lockhart's hands?

Now that she'd had time to think about it, Casey wasn't particularly surprised that Janice trusted Steve that much. Steve was well-known around the airport for his kindness, his impulsive generosity, and his loyalty to his employees. He was a man people instinctively liked. Casey didn't actually dislike him, though he irritated her to no end with his incessant teasing. Mostly, he worried her. His charter service was growing quickly and though not yet as well established as Jansen Charter Service, he was beginning to cut into her customer base. Each time he seduced one of her clients away from her, she found her own self-doubt growing.

What if it were true that she wasn't qualified to run the business her father and his father before him had managed so successfully? What if she really was too young and inexperienced? What if her father had been right to have so little faith in her...?

"You've drifted off again," Edward said. "Casey, really, if there's something seriously wrong...if you need anything from me..."

She shook her head. "No. I'm sorry, I guess I'm just a little tired."

Which, of course, only gave him a new reason to fuss. "You aren't getting enough rest. And not enough fun. You're too young to spend all your time working. Most women your age go to parties and out on dates, or are starting their families. You don't even make time to see anyone outside of the office."

"I see *you*," she reminded him, trying to sidestep the all-too-familiar discussion she knew was coming.

He shook his head stubbornly. "I'm your brother. I'm talking about other men. Don't tell me you don't want a family—I know you better than that."

Warmed as always that he considered himself her brother despite the fragility of the connection, Casey responded in a softer tone. "Of course I want a family, Edward. And I'll have one, someday, if I'm lucky."

A sudden mental picture of herself holding little Annie while the baby had taken her bottle made her heart ache. She really did want children of her own someday. She had simply been forced to postpone that goal when her father's untimely illness and death had changed her life so drastically. She shook her head to clear the images. "As you pointed out, I'm still young. There's plenty of time for that sort of thing when I've got everything cleared away at JCS. It's only been a year since Dad died, and there were so many of his affairs to settle...but I've almost done that now. It won't be much longer before I'll be able to take some time off for myself."

She was bluffing, of course. JCS was still far from being back on solid financial ground, and it wasn't helping that Steve kept luring her clients away from her. But how could she admit defeat now, when JCS was all she had left of her father and her grandfather? When she was the only Jansen left to ensure its survival? Couldn't Edward understand how important that was to her?

No, of course he couldn't. His own father had died so early that Edward had never known what it was like to work constantly for a father's approval. Nor did he know how it felt to be always aware of a father's disappointment. Louis Jansen had always made it clear that he had wanted a son, and had been disappointed that his stepson had shown no interest in the business Louis had nurtured so passionately. Casey had definitely been his last alternative when it was time to turn that business over to someone else, and she'd been aware that he had done so without a great deal of optimism that she would be able to keep it afloat.

She cleared her throat again. "Really, Edward, everything is fine," she repeated. "Tell me more about the lieutenant governor's root canal."

Even though she'd rather be enduring a root canal than hearing the minute details of one, she made an effort to concentrate on Edward's story. Edward's work was important to him, she reminded herself. And she would show interest in it because he was important to her.

Besides, she added silently, it gave her an excuse to concentrate on something besides worrying about how Steve was getting along with Annie.

STEVE HAD WALKED the hallway of his house so many times it was a wonder he hadn't worn a path into the carpet. Held snugly in his arms, wrapped in a soft plaid stadium blanket, Annie slept soundly and apparently contentedly. She wasn't fooling him for a minute. No matter how deeply asleep she appeared, he knew if he even tried to lay her down, she'd scream her tiny lungs out. He knew because he'd been trying to put her down for more than an hour now.

His arms were getting tired, not from her weight, which was negligible, but from being held too long in the same position. He was hungry, since he had intended to eat after he put her to bed. And he needed to go to the bathroom.

He was sheepishly aware that his entire evening was being controlled by a six-pound infant, but there didn't seem to be much he could do about it at the moment. He'd told Casey he could handle this, and he was a long way from admitting defeat.

Maybe if he held Annie in his left arm, he could use his right hand to eat a sandwich or something while he paced. As far as going to the bathroom with her—no way.

His doorbell chimed musically through the quiet house, startling the baby and making her jolt, proving his suspicion that she hadn't been as soundly asleep as she had appeared. Steve glanced at his watch. Just before 10:00 p.m. He couldn't imagine who would stop by at this hour without calling first.

Unless...

He strode swiftly across the room and, cradling Annie in his left arm, used his right hand to jerk the door open. "Oh," he said, a bit surprised but hardly disappointed. "It's you."

Her arms loaded with packages, Casey frowned at him. "You were expecting someone else?"

"When the doorbell rang, I thought maybe Janice had come for the baby," he admitted.

Her frown deepened. "No word from her yet?"

He shook his head. "B.J.'s been looking all evening. He called and said no one has seen her since last weekend." He moved out of the doorway to give her room to pass him. "Come in."

"I brought some things for the baby. I didn't know if you had a chance to get anything."

Annie was still wearing the little white shirt they'd found her in, and he was down to a handful of disposable diapers. He smiled gratefully at Casey, both surprised and pleased by her unexpected gesture. "I really appreciate this. Thanks."

Casey set the bags on his oak coffee table, then turned to face him. "You look ragged."

Trust Casey not to mince words. "The kid has a way of expressing her opinions."

Looking a bit uncertain, she ran her hands down her sides, making Steve realize that she had changed clothes since he'd last seen her. She now wore a thin, sleeveless black top over loose black pants with strappy black sandals. The kind of outfit she would wear on a date, he thought with a quick frown. A frown that disappeared when he realized she must have cut the date short to come check on him and Annie.

"Is there anything I can do to help?" she asked.

He promptly took her up on her tentative offer. "You can hold her for a few minutes while I grab a sandwich or something. She hasn't let me put her down since I got home with her, and I'm starving."

"Oh. Okay, sure." She reached for the baby.

Standing close to make the transfer, Steve became aware of her subtly floral scent. She'd pinned her long hair up, baring the back of her neck. He resisted a quick impulse to find out if that exposed skin was as soft and silky as it looked. "Your appointment ended early?"

"It was just for dinner," she replied carelessly, looking down at the baby, who squirmed for a moment, then settled into her arms. "Have you tried rocking Annie to sleep?"

"I've tried *everything*. The only way to keep her quiet is to hold her and walk with her. I've logged a dozen miles or more up and down my hallway."

"When did she eat last?"

"She took a little formula about an hour ago. Her last full bottle was the one you gave her nearly four hours ago."

"Maybe she'll take a little more now and go to sleep. Where's the bottle?"

"I'll get it." He turned and headed for the kitchen, aware that Casey followed him. Fortunately the kitchen was fairly neat for a change, he noted in a quick, assessing glance. He popped the bottle in the microwave to knock the chill off, then turned to Casey. "There's a rocking chair in the living room."

"I'll sit in here with her and keep you company while you eat." She settled carefully in one of the bow-back chairs at the round oak pedestal table.

Steve wondered if she really wanted to keep him company or if she was just nervous about being alone with the baby. He handed her the slightly warmed bottle, watching as she offered it to Annie. The baby squirmed and fussed before beginning to nurse—slowly at first, then with more enthusiasm.

"Apparently, she prefers it when you feed her," Steve commented, aware only then that both he and Casey had been holding their breath.

"Maybe she wasn't really hungry earlier. She's probably confused and unsettled about everything that has happened to her today."

Steve pushed a hand through his hair. "I can certainly empathize with that."

"I'm sure you can."

He edged toward the door. "If you'll excuse me just a minute, I have to—um—wash my hands."

Casey nodded matter-of-factly, looking more comfortable with the baby now. "Take your time. We'll be fine."

He wasn't gone long. He was still surprised that Casey had come, which he told her when he returned to the kitchen and opened the refrigerator. "How did you get my address?"

"I called Madelyn," she admitted. "I couldn't stop worrying that there were things you needed for Annie. You were so adamant about no one else finding out about this that I was concerned you wouldn't call anyone for help."

He set out bread, lunch meat, cheese, lettuce, tomato and mustard. "Want a sandwich?"

"No, thank you. I just finished dinner."

He wondered who she'd gone out with. For whom she had changed into the flattering pantsuit, dabbed on perfume and pinned up her hair. "I hope Annie and I haven't ruined your evening."

"No. I had no plans after dinner with my stepbrother."

Her stepbrother. Steve smiled and relaxed. "How about something to drink? Soda? Coffee? Tea? I have Earl Grey or herbal."

"Herbal tea sounds good. It's too late for caffeine."

He set water on to boil while he assembled his sandwich on a paper plate, dumping a handful of chips on the side. By the time his makeshift meal was ready, so was the tea. He carried everything to the table, where Casey was trying to pat a burp out of the baby. When she had succeeded, she settled Annie back into her arms and offered the bottle again. "She really was hungry."

"I swear I tried to feed her," Steve said, settling into a chair. "She wouldn't have it."

A quick smile curved Casey's mouth. "Maybe she was waiting to dine with you."

"That was very thoughtful of you, Annie," he said gravely. "But next time, don't bother, okay?"

He liked seeing Casey across his kitchen table while he ate. The overhead lighting gleamed in her upswept brown hair, making his fingers itch to pull out the pins and watch it tumble to the middle of her back. Her lipstick had faded, leaving her sexy, full lips moist and natural, stirring a hunger in him his sandwich had no chance of satisfying. As often as he'd fantasized about having her here like this, he hadn't expected it to happen so soon.

Of course, his fantasies hadn't included the baby in her arms. He didn't try to delude himself that she was here for any other reason. "You were worried about the baby, weren't you?"

She glanced at him with a lifted eyebrow. "Of course. Why else would I be here?"

Why else, indeed. He reminded himself that she saw him as an annoying business rival, not as a friend. And certainly not as anything more. *For now.* "It was very nice of you to come by and check on us. Of course, I *was* handling it," he couldn't resist pointing out.

Her smile was wry. "Of course you were. Which is why you're wolfing that sandwich down as if you haven't eaten in days."

He chuckled. "I didn't say it was easy."

She looked down at the baby again, biting her

lower lip and causing him to squirm. After a moment, he asked, "What's bothering you, Casey?"

Her eyes were wide when she looked up. "What do you think?"

"We'll find Janice. I know a guy I can maybe call to help—a P.I. He owes me a favor. I flew him out of a tight spot once."

That got her attention. "You really think he can find Janice?"

"If anyone can find her, it's Blake. I'll call him tomorrow, if we haven't heard anything."

"And the baby?"

"I'll take care of her." He watched Casey swallow, and wished just once she'd look a bit more confident when he said that.

The telephone rang just as he was about to assure her again that Annie would be fine. Steve snatched the kitchen receiver before the ringing could disturb the baby, who was just finishing her bottle. "H'lo?" he asked, expecting to hear Madelyn or B.J. reply.

Instead, there was a long pause and then a whispered, "Is the baby okay?"

Steve froze. He forced himself to answer calmly. "The baby is fine. Where are you?"

A sob was the only answer.

"I haven't called the authorities," he said reassuringly. "No one outside the company knows I have the baby." Technically, Casey wasn't in his company, but since Janice worked for Casey, too, he didn't see much difference.

A gasp of gratitude was followed by a choked, "Thank you. I knew you would help me."

"I could help you more if you'd tell me what's wrong. Why don't you come here? Or if you like, I'll come to you."

"No. I—not yet. Soon. I promise. I'll come for her soon. Don't—please don't call anyone yet."

"I won't turn her in," he vowed rashly, deeply affected by the desperate misery in the young mother's voice. "But you have to—"

"Thank you. I'm sorry, I have to go. I'll call soon. Kiss—kiss Annie for me." The break in her voice was heartrending.

"Janice—"

But she was gone. A dial tone buzzed in his ear.

"Damn." Steve hung up the phone and turned to find Casey on her feet, the dozing baby clutched to her chest.

"That was Janice?"

He nodded.

"Where is she? What's happening? Why did she leave the baby? When is she—?"

Steve held up a hand. "I can't answer any of your questions. She didn't tell me anything."

"What did she say?"

"She asked about the baby and begged me not to turn her in. And then she hung up."

Casey rocked Annie gently in her arms, her expression so troubled that Steve wondered if she was trying to soothe the baby or herself. "This is crazy. I can't believe what we're doing. Annie deserves better than this. She needs a stable home. A mother who is there for her, and can support her and take care of her. Even if Janice comes back, how is she going to get by on the small salary she makes cleaning our offices? Who's going to take care of Annie while Janice works?"

"We'll help her. There's assistance available for single mothers with financial problems. You know Janice. She's a hardworking young woman. Once she settles whatever trouble she's in now, she'll do the right thing by her baby."

Casey sighed and shook her head. "I know you have a reputation for being fiercely loyal to your friends and employees, but I never thought of you as naive."

"I'm not naive. I consider myself a very good judge of character, actually. I've rarely been burned by someone I trusted."

She didn't seem overly reassured. "You're impulsive and unconventional and reckless. It's no wonder Janice assumed you wouldn't do the sensible thing and call the authorities as soon as you found this baby in your plane."

Genuinely amused by her summary of his character, Steve chuckled. "I like you, too, Casey, darlin'."

Her cheeks went pink. Abruptly, she turned away from him. "We should try putting Annie to bed. Do you have a place for her to sleep?"

"Yeah. I borrowed a bassinet from my neighbor. I told her I was baby-sitting for a sick friend."

"And she bought that?"

"Why not? It's the truth, in a way. For all we know, Janice *is* sick and that's why she can't take care of Annie right now."

"I brought a couple of sleepers. Let's get her changed and then maybe she'll settle down for the night."

Very carefully, trying not to jostle the baby awake, they eased her into a clean diaper and one of the soft, one-piece cotton sleepers Casey had brought with her. The garment was pink, embroidered with tiny flowers on the collar. Digging in the bags Casey had carried in, Steve found three more comfortable-looking outfits, tiny booties, two lightweight baby blankets, a colorful plastic rattle and a whimsical little terry-cloth teddy bear. "You had quite a shopping spree," he said with a smile.

"I grabbed a few things in the baby department at the Wal-Mart near here," she replied with a slightly self-conscious shrug. "I didn't know exactly what you needed, but this seemed like a good start."

"It really was very thoughtful of you."

"I did it for Annie."

"I never thought anything else," he assured her.

She nodded, as if satisfied that she'd made her point. "Why don't you try putting her to bed now?"

"Why don't I?" He couldn't help teasing Casey a bit. Her somewhat bossy attitude didn't bother him;

he knew she reacted that way when she was feeling threatened or uncertain. He picked up the baby with exaggerated care, and tiptoed into his bedroom, where he'd set up the wicker bassinet.

Casey followed him. "Put her on her back," she whispered. "The experts say that's the safest position. And make sure there aren't any blankets around her face. She's too little to push away anything that's impeding her breathing."

Moments later, Steve and Casey stood side-by-side next to the bassinet, holding their breath as Annie squirmed and mewed and then settled into sleep. Steve released his breath slowly when it became apparent that the baby was going to stay down this time—at least for a while. He couldn't resist looping an arm around Casey's shoulders. "She really is a sweetheart, isn't she?"

Casey stepped back a bit too quickly, causing his arm to fall to his side. "Yes," she murmured. "Um— I'd better go."

With one last glance at the sleeping baby, he followed Casey out of his room. "What's your hurry, darlin'?"

"It's getting late. I need to go home. And stop calling me that!" she said, her nerves obviously beginning to fray. "We're competitors, not friends. Just because I'm as concerned about this baby as you are doesn't mean I've forgotten you're trying to put me out of business."

He couldn't help chuckling a little. "I'm not trying

to put you out of business, Casey. I happen to think there's enough opportunity for both of us."

"Then quit stealing my customers," she snapped. "Find your own."

"I'm not actively campaigning to steal your customers. But I won't refuse them when they come to me, either."

She couldn't seem to think of an appropriate response to that. She snatched up her purse and moved toward the door. "Is there anything else I can do—for the baby?" she added.

An idea occurred to him, but he knew it would take nerve to ask. Of course, nerve had never been something he'd lacked. "As a matter of fact, there is something you can do for us..."

"What?"

"Are you by any chance free to baby-sit tomorrow? I have flight school to teach in the morning and two lessons to give tomorrow afternoon."

She gaped at him. "You're asking me to baby-sit so you can go to work? After all we just said?"

"I'd certainly appreciate it. I thought about asking Madelyn to help, but she takes care of her invalid mother on the weekends, and I'm not sure she can handle both the baby and her mother. I could ask my neighbor, but again I worry about the explanations I'd have to make."

Casey let out a gusty sigh. "I can't believe this."

"Well, you did ask if there was anything you could do. If you have other plans, I understand..."

"I was planning to spend tomorrow at home catching up on paperwork. I suppose I could do some of it here."

He smiled. "Sure you could."

She frowned at him. "I can't believe I'm even considering this. What time do you need me to be here?"

"Nine o'clock? Flight school starts at nine-thirty. That'll give me just enough time to get to the airport. My last lesson's at one, so I should be home by two-thirty."

She nodded. "Don't dawdle getting back."

She sounded like a schoolmarm. It was all Steve could do not to grin, but he knew when *not* to push his luck. "I won't."

She threw the strap of her purse over her shoulder and reached for the doorknob. "If you steal any of my clients tomorrow while I'm here baby-sitting for you, I swear I'll skin you alive."

"Now, Casey, just how low do you think I am?"

The look she gave him suggested she thought him somewhat lower than a snake's belly. He didn't take offense. Casey was feeling a little stressed right now, and she needed someone to blame. He supposed he made a handy target.

"You still have my number if you need me tonight? Or if you hear any more from Janice?"

He recited the number without referring to the paper she'd written it on earlier.

Casey grimaced. "I'm definitely changing my number first thing next week."

He laughed and traced her jaw with the fingertips of his right hand. "I don't think that will be necessary. Thanks again for the stuff, Casey. And for helping out tomorrow."

She left with a murmur he didn't quite understand.

He was smiling when he shut the door behind her. He knew she'd convinced herself that she'd only dropped by because of the baby. But she wouldn't have come and spent so much time with him if she really disliked him as much as she pretended—would she?

CASEY WAS ANNOYED to find herself touching her jaw with her left hand as she guided her steering wheel with her right. She could almost feel her skin tingling where Steve had caressed it—which was utterly ridiculous, of course.

She was *not* attracted to Steve Lockhart, she assured herself. Okay, so maybe she was a little, but that was only hormones. The natural reaction of a healthy, romance-deprived woman to a virile, extraordinarily good-looking male. She had no intention of acting on those unwelcome feelings. The only reason she'd chased him at the airport today was to yell at him for stealing her business. And the only reason she'd gone to his house this evening was to make sure the baby was all right.

As for why she'd agreed to spend tomorrow at his house so he could work, well...mark that off to temporary insanity. Even if she *was* attracted to Steve—a little attracted—there was no way on earth she was doing anything about it. The guy drove her crazy— and not just because he had dimples that flashed every time he grinned. Which was entirely too often for her peace of mind.

He was insolent. Cocky. Lackadaisical. He seemed to have an almost pathological aversion to following rules. Take this present situation, for example. Any normal businessman would have freaked out at finding a newborn baby in his airplane. He'd have immediately contacted the police and washed his hands of the entire situation.

Not Steve. He'd taken the baby home and prom- ised the troubled mother he would handle every- thing. Knowing nothing about babies, without any supplies or assistance, he'd made himself responsi- ble. Any number of things could go wrong, but was he worried? He certainly didn't act like it.

A tiny voice inside her whispered that Steve was the kind of friend one could count on through thick and thin, someone whose loyalty far surpassed his own self-interests. Admirable in some ways, she supposed, but undeniably rash. She was no risk- taker and never had been—until today, when Steve and his employees had made her feel like a heartless villain for even considering turning Annie over to child welfare services.

She drove into her garage and killed the engine of her sensible sedan. She was tired—close to exhaustion—but she doubted she would sleep a wink. She was far more likely to lie awake all night worrying about a troubled young mother and a baby whose fate lay in Steve Lockhart's big, strong hands.

4

BY NINE O'CLOCK the next morning, Steve might have gotten five hours of sleep. Maybe. He wished someone had warned him that babies were nocturnal creatures whose idea of a long period of rest was a two-hour stretch. Judging from Annie's behavior, babies slept in snatches, wanted to be fed and held whenever they were awake, were unable to tolerate a damp diaper for more than a few minutes, and seemed to enjoy testing just how much noise their tiny lungs could generate.

He thought of recent news reports of women who gave birth to six or eight babies at a time, and he wondered how the parents kept their sanity. Just one night with this *one* baby had exhausted him.

There was no way, of course, that he was going to let Casey know the night hadn't been a snap. He was smiling when he opened the door to her. "Good morning, Casey. Did you sleep well?"

"Better than you did, apparently," she replied, studying him with narrowed eyes. "Problems?"

So much for fooling her. He hadn't realized she was quite so perceptive. "No, everything's fine. Annie just doesn't believe in getting all her sleep in one block. She likes to break it into two or three hour intervals—and I don't go back to sleep as easily as she does."

Casey walked past him into the entryway, her long hair swaying with her movements and making Steve aware of how nice she looked in her pale blue scoop-neck T-shirt and loose jeans. He rarely saw her dressed so casually. He liked it—but then he also liked seeing her in her prim working clothes.

"You're sure you're up to flying today?" she asked, breaking into his appreciative survey of her appearance. "You wouldn't be dumb enough to go up with student pilots if you weren't in top form, would you?"

"As much as I appreciate your confidence and your concern, Casey, darlin', I'm fine. I don't need a lot of sleep."

She set down her purse and a bulging briefcase, then turned to look at him again. "You've had breakfast?"

"Coffee, orange juice, a bowl of cereal and a bagel." He couldn't resist reaching out to rub her cheek with his knuckles in a teasingly affectionate gesture. "Is that healthy enough to satisfy you?"

She almost stumbled in her haste to back away from him. "I'm only concerned about your students. They should have the security of an instructor who is well-rested and alert."

"And they'll have that security." He wasn't sure whether to be annoyed or amused by her prissy tone.

It seemed easier to settle for amusement, especially since she'd blushed so intriguingly when he'd touched her. "And did *you* have a good night's rest and a nourishing breakfast? Trust me, you need to be in top shape for your day, as well."

"I'm sure I can handle it. Is Annie sleeping now?"

He nodded. "She's in the bassinet in my room. She'll let you know when she wants to get up. There are several filled bottles in the fridge—all you have to do is pop one in the microwave for about a minute. She likes her formula at about room temperature. Diapers are stacked on my dresser, next to her clean sleepers."

She nodded. If she was nervous about baby-sitting for the day, she didn't let it show. "What about Janice? Are you going to do anything about finding her today?"

"I'll make a few calls when I get some extra time. I thought I'd ask the local hospitals if a Janice Gibson has checked in any time during the past week."

"Good idea. What about that P.I. friend you mentioned?"

"I thought we'd wait the rest of the day before we call him in. Janice is likely to show up at any time to pick up the baby, and I don't want to get too many people involved unless it's necessary."

She looked worried, but nodded. "You'd better go or you'll be late."

"Help yourself to anything in the kitchen, okay? There are soft drinks and fruit juice in the refrigerator. And you should be able to find something for lunch."

"I'll manage. Now go. And come back as soon as you can. I have errands to run this afternoon."

He wondered if her brusque tone was intended to mask her uncertainty about being responsible for little Annie for the next few hours. He had to give her credit for courage. He knew she was no more experienced with infants than he was, but she wasn't letting her insecurity show.

Because he admired her nerve, and because he had wanted to for so very long, anyway, he stopped fighting the impulse to kiss her. He moved so quickly she didn't have a chance to evade him, his mouth settling on hers before she could realize what he intended to do. And the kiss was as delicious as he'd always expected it to be—until Casey abruptly pulled back with a gasp.

Since she seemed unable to speak for the moment, he stepped back and said as casually as if he routinely kissed her goodbye, "I have to be going. Call if you need me."

"I—don't do that again!" she said, but he was already halfway out of the room and could pretend he hadn't heard her.

It was with some reluctance that Steve left for the airport. As much as he enjoyed his work, he would rather have stayed home that day for the rare chance to spend time alone with Casey Jansen.

THE MINUTE CASEY HEARD Steve's car leave the driveway, she sagged against the front door. He had kissed her! Without as much as a word of warning, he'd simply pulled her close and planted one on her—completely emptying her mind of coherent thought. What on earth had made him do that? And why on earth had it taken her so long to push him away?

What was she doing here, anyway? She wasn't qualified to take care of a helpless infant! She was probably breaking laws and risking her professional reputation by conspiring with Steve to keep Janice's actions quiet. And, most unbelievable of all, she was actually *helping* Steve compete against her business by baby-sitting today so he could go to work. Now he probably thought she was doing so because his famous charm had gotten to her, rather than her own soft heart where Annie was concerned.

She could only assume that the shock of finding the baby had temporarily robbed her of her common sense.

She ran both hands through her hair, letting out a long, unsteady breath. Okay, she was here. Might as well get busy. She should probably check on the baby before setting up her laptop and paperwork. Anything to keep her busy, to keep her from remembering that staggeringly unexpected kiss.

Annie was sleeping, lying on her back in the pretty wicker bassinet, her pink face relaxed, her rosy mouth pursing in an occasional suckling motion. So

tiny, Casey thought, her throat tightening. So totally
dependent on the adults around her. What had Janice been thinking? What had driven her to this act
of desperation? What was going to happen—to any
of them?

But standing here worrying wasn't accomplishing
anything. She tiptoed out of the bedroom to the living room, picked up her briefcase and looked for a
place to set up. In one corner of the casually-
furnished room was a small, round oak table sur-
rounded by four cushioned oak chairs—a corner she
suspected had seen a few friendly poker games. She
could have set up her computer in the kitchen or dining room, but she chose this table, instead. It was
close to the hallway that led to the bedrooms, so she
wouldn't have to worry about not hearing Annie.
And she was comfortable in this room.

She liked Steve's house. She hadn't paid much attention to it last night, being more concerned with
Annie's welfare and Janice's whereabouts, but she
had time now to look around a bit. Just superficially,
of course—she was no snoop. He'd decorated with
heavy oak furniture and nubby plaid fabrics, a masculine effect, but not overwhelmingly so. The art-
work that graced his walls depicted wildlife
scenes—flying ducks, grazing deer, prowling
wolves.

The bedroom in which Annie was sleeping carried
the same oak, plaid and wildlife theme. Casey was
unable to resist taking a quick walk through the rest

of the house before settling down to work. There were two spare bedrooms, one furnished very sparsely and looking as though it was rarely entered, the other apparently used as Steve's home office, containing a desk, computer, fax, copy machine and several filing cabinets. She didn't go into that room, telling herself that nothing in there was any of her concern.

The dining room was decorated with hunting prints and featured a Williamsburg chandelier over a maple dining table with six matching chairs. A bowfront china cabinet held gold-rimmed white china and gold-accented crystal glasses. Something about this room made Casey think of heirlooms. Had these things been passed down from Steve's mother or grandmother? She hadn't thought of him as the sentimental type, but considering his loyalty to his employees, she supposed he was.

The last room she glanced into was the kitchen with its oak cabinets, oak pedestal table and terra cotta tile floor. It was as comfortable and neat as she remembered it last night.

She wondered if someone had helped him decorate. Everything was so well coordinated—not fancy, but pleasantly harmonious. She probably would have changed a few things, of course. Toned down the wildlife theme, added a few frills and pillows. But the house seemed to reflect Steve's personality—so well, in fact, that she felt his presence everywhere she turned. Which didn't contribute to her peace of mind.

What was it about the guy that made just being in his house an unsettling experience? And if she was as indifferent to him as she'd always tried to be, why did just wandering through the rooms he lived in make her nerves go all tingly?

"Stop being ridiculous, Casey, and get to work," she muttered.

She had just sat down at her computer when Annie woke up.

It was the last time she attempted to work that day.

STEVE HAD JUST FINISHED his second and final flying lesson and was locking his office in preparation to go home when a burly man approached from the nearly-empty parking lot. "I'm looking for the owner of this operation," he said. "Is that you?"

Before answering, Steve took a moment to study the guy. He appeared to be in his late forties. His dark hair was slicked back from his broad face with too much gel, and his neck was so thick his ears seemed to blend into his wide shoulders. "I'm Steve Lockhart. What can I do for you?"

"I'm trying to find someone who might be an employee of yours. Her name is Janice Gibson."

Steve managed not to react to the name except for lifting one eyebrow. "Janice Gibson?"

The guy nodded. "I've been told she works for you."

Was this man the reason Janice was so afraid? Deciding to give away nothing until he knew exactly what was going on, Steve crossed his arms and eyed the other man dispassionately. "Janice Gibson was an employee for a few months, but she no longer works for me."

"Did you fire her?"

"She quit."

"When?"

Though he wasn't usually the type to make snap judgments about people, Steve had already decided he didn't like this guy. "Recently. I'm sorry, there's nothing more I can tell you. I have no idea of Ms. Gibson's present location."

Which was the truth, of course. He saw no reason to mention the baby at this point.

"What about the other company she worked for here? Jansen Charter Service? Think anyone there would know anything?"

"Casey Jansen and I talked about this only yesterday. She hasn't heard from Janice, either. We're both planning to hire someone to replace her early next week. We assume Janice has left the area."

The guy looked at Steve suspiciously. "You're sure you don't know how to reach her?"

"No. I don't."

The sincerity in his voice must have been convincing. The other man's frown deepened. "Hell." After a moment, he pushed his hands into his pockets. "If you hear from her, will you let me know? My name's Frank Claybrook and I'm staying at the Discount Inn on Ninth Street."

"I don't expect to hear from Janice, but if I do, why should I call you? What do you want with her?"

"Let's just say it's a family matter," Claybrook answered flatly. "It's very important that I find her."

Steve shrugged, not at all swayed by the vague explanation. "I really can't help you. She was just someone who cleaned my offices, not a personal friend."

Claybrook hesitated a moment, then nodded curtly. "You know where to reach me if you hear anything. I'll be there for a couple more days. By the way, there's a chance of a nice reward for anyone who can lead me to her."

No amount of reward could have enticed Steve to betray Janice—or anyone else to whom he'd pledged his loyalty. He merely glanced at his watch. "If you'll excuse me, I have an appointment."

Without a word, Claybrook stepped aside. Steve could feel the guy's gaze on the back of his neck until he climbed into his car and drove away. Just to be on the safe side—and telling himself he was probably being paranoid—he made sure he wasn't followed as he drove home.

After entering his house a half hour later, Steve took one look at Casey and decided that if he'd looked half as frazzled that morning, it was no wonder she'd known immediately about his rough night. She was pacing when he walked in, the baby on her shoulder, her formerly fresh clothes now wrinkled and disheveled. She'd kicked off her loafers, revealing pale blue socks that matched her T-shirt.

"She won't let me put her down," she said when she saw Steve. "I've been walking up and down the hallway for the past hour."

His first instinct was to take her in his arms and offer comfort. Maybe another kiss. Or two. Or more.

Knowing she wouldn't appreciate that, he offered commiseration, instead. "I did the same thing last night," he admitted.

"I tried putting her in the carrier where she could watch me work and she wouldn't have it. I put her in the bassinet, thinking she would cry herself to sleep, but she screamed for twenty solid minutes without letting up. I couldn't stand it anymore. The only time she's quiet is when I'm rocking her or walking with her."

"I know. She wants to be held. Maybe she's feeling insecure because her mother isn't here."

"My arms are starting to cramp."

"Here, let me take her. Is it time for her next bottle?"

"I fed her just before we started pacing the hallway. She shouldn't need to eat again for a while."

He took the baby and settled her into his arms. She fussed a moment, then quieted when he began to rock her gently. "I think she's getting spoiled."

"I think you're right. I wonder if a pacifier would comfort her? I know they're controversial and Janice might not appreciate us getting Annie attached to one, but it seems like she needs something to soothe her."

"I hadn't even thought of a pacifier. Maybe we should try one. I'm not morally opposed to them, are you?"

"After today, I'd try just about anything," she confessed, rubbing her forehead. "Who would have thought a baby this small could be so vocal in her demands?"

He chuckled and patted Annie's back. "She's a pistol, all right."

Casey cocked her head and looked at him as if suddenly recovering enough from her own distress to notice something. "Did something happen at work today?"

Steve kept his gaze on the baby. "What do you mean?"

"Something's bothering you. Have you heard from Janice again?"

For someone who claimed to dislike him, Casey was certainly able to read him well. "I haven't heard from Janice. But something *did* happen that caused me to be concerned about her."

"I knew it. What happened? Is she all right? Is she...?"

"Casey." He broke in with a slight smile. "Why

don't we move into the kitchen for this? I could use something cold to drink."

Fifteen minutes later, Steve had emptied a can of soda and told Casey every detail of his encounter with the weird guy outside his office. He could have described the incident more concisely, but Casey kept interrupting with questions.

"Who do you think he was? What do you think he wants with Janice? Did he know about the baby?"

Leaning against the counter, holding his soda can in his right hand and the baby in the crook of his left arm, Steve shook his head. "I don't know. He didn't..."

Casey gasped. "You don't suppose *he's* the baby's father, do you?"

"No, I don't. He's a good twenty-five years older than Janice. And I didn't get the impression there was a personal relationship between them. My guess would be that he's trying to find her for someone else."

Her eyes widened even more. "You mean he's, like, a pro? Someone who wants to hurt her?"

"Now don't let your imagination run away with you," he admonished, rather amused.

"You said Janice sounded frightened. She begged you to protect her baby. Maybe she's...maybe she's gotten tangled up with the Mafia or something."

He had to chuckle at that. "Now you really are getting carried away. What would the Mafia be doing here? We're in a dry county, there's no gambling and we roll up the streets at 10:00 p.m. Hardly a den of iniquity."

"We don't know where Janice came from before she showed up looking for work," she reminded him, her tone expressing resentment that he wasn't taking her seriously.

"I'll admit she seems to be running from something, and I didn't trust the guy who was asking about her. But until we know what's going on, it doesn't do any good to make up scenarios."

Annie made one of her funny little noises and Steve shifted her to a new position. The kid really didn't like to be still very long, he thought wryly.

Casey was wearing her worried frown again. She leaned her elbows on the table, resting her chin on her fists. "What are we going to do now?"

"You said you had some errands to run this afternoon. Feel free to leave whenever you're ready."

She shook her head impatiently. "I didn't mean that. What are we going to do about Janice? And the baby? Don't you think we should consider calling the police now?"

Actually, Steve was even more opposed to calling the police now than he'd been when they'd first found the baby. He didn't like the thought that someone was trying to intimidate one of his employees. He hadn't liked the guy who'd interrogated him outside his office. And he would be damned if he would turn little Annie over to a bunch of bureaucrats without first doing all he could to help her and her mother. "No police."

"What about your P.I. friend? If someone else has been hired to find Janice, why can't we do the same?"

That was certainly a viable option. If anyone could locate a missing person, it would be Blake. "I'll try to reach him. If he's available, he might agree to help us out."

"You're sure that Claybrook guy didn't know you have the baby?"

"I told you, the baby never came up."

"You'll probably accuse me of letting my imagination run away with me again, but...is it possible he followed you here?"

"No, it isn't possible. I kept one eye on my rear-view mirror the entire way."

"So it *did* occur to you."

He nodded. "As much as I hate to admit it, it did occur to me."

"Of course, he could probably find your address in the phone book. Unless your number is unlisted?"

"Why would I have an unlisted number? I've never had a problem with unwanted calls. By the way, why is *your* number unlisted?"

"It just seemed like a prudent step for a single woman to take."

"Hmm. And if any single guys are interested in calling you?"

She leveled a look at him. "When I want someone to call me, I give him my number."

He grinned. "I know. And I still have it memorized."

"I did not—" She stopped, drew a deep breath and glared at him. "Stop baiting me. We have real problems to discuss. You just said you're in the phone book and easy to locate. What if...?"

"Casey, there's no reason to think the guy would be interested in finding me at all. As far as he knows, I'm simply someone Janice used to work for. He has no reason to think I'm connected to her in any other way."

She chewed her lip. After a moment, she said, "I really think you should call your friend. I was already worried about Janice, but this—this scares me."

He moved across the room, still cradling Annie in his left arm, and ran his right hand down Casey's long, silky hair. Though he had intended the gesture to be reassuring, he enjoyed it so much he did it again—for himself that time. "Don't be scared, Casey, darlin'."

She immediately straightened her shoulders. "I'm not scared for myself. I'm worried about Janice and the baby."

"Don't be scared for them, either. I'm going to make sure no one hurts either of them."

She eyed him doubtfully. He was aware that, for the first time, she wasn't automatically moving away from his touch. He didn't flatter himself that she was growing fonder of him. She was probably just too distracted to pay much attention to his actions. But it was nice to stand close to her and feel like they were in this together.

As reluctant as he was for her to leave, he didn't like seeing the lines of strain around her pretty mouth. Maybe she needed to get out for a while after being cooped up here with the baby most of the day. "Go run your errands, Casey. I'll watch out for Annie."

She nodded slowly. "I do have a few things I have to do. But I'll come back later this evening. You're getting low on formula. I'll pick some up while I'm out. And I'll bring you dinner. I know it's difficult to prepare something for yourself while you're trying to keep Annie happy at the same time."

He almost told her that wasn't necessary. He could always call for a pizza or something. But he couldn't resist the opportunity to spend a bit more time with her. "I really appreciate that. Let me give you some money for supplies. You've already bought clothes and diapers."

She lifted her chin in a proud gesture. "No, thank you. I haven't spent that much."

Something in her expression warned him not to argue with her. He would figure out a way to pay her back later, he decided.

He walked her to the front door, noticing that she looked warily up and down the quiet residential street before stepping outside. The fact that a stranger was looking for Janice had obviously spooked her. He wished he could assure her that the incident hadn't worried him at all—and he wished even more that it were true.

"I really appreciate you helping me out this morning, Casey."

She looked down at her hands. "You're welcome," she said, a bit gruffly.

He leaned closer to her, wondering if there was any chance of stealing another kiss.

But Casey was onto him now. She sidestepped him quickly, giving him a look of warning. "I have to go. I'll see you later," she said.

He sighed in resignation and nodded, letting her leave without further comment.

"Well, Annie," he said when he and the baby were alone again. "How'd you like to try sitting in your seat for a few minutes? I need to make a couple of phone calls."

Annie wasn't happy about being put down. She cried and flailed her arms and legs. Just as Steve was about to give up and hold her again, she fell asleep in midwail. He hovered over her a few minutes, until he was sure she was really asleep. Only then did he tiptoe into the kitchen to make his calls.

AFTER RUNNING HER ERRANDS and checking in with her office, Casey stopped by her apartment to do a load of laundry and water her houseplants. She thought about making something to take to Steve's for dinner later, but decided to stop for takeout instead. She had cans of formula, more diapers and a few other baby supplies in her car. She'd bought a bottle of baby soap while she was at it. As far as she knew, Steve hadn't had the nerve to try bathing Annie yet, and neither had she. One or both of them were going to have to make the attempt tonight.

It was almost six when she picked up her purse and headed for the door. By the time she stopped for food and arrived at Steve's house, he would probably be ready to eat. She was only doing these things for him because he was taking care of the baby, she assured herself. Even if it turned out that he'd been misguided in his decision to take care of Annie rather than turn her over to the authorities, it was really rather sweet of him to be doing so much. What other bachelor would be so willing to take full responsibility for the infant daughter of a woman he hardly knew?

She had just reached for her doorknob when the telephone rang. She almost let the answering machine pick it up. Only the thought that it could be Steve with a last-minute request made her answer. "Hello?"

"Casey Jansen?" The voice was unfamiliar.

"Yes?"

"My name is Walter Park. I'm trying to locate a woman I believe was on your payroll for a time. Her name is Janice Gibson."

Casey's fingers went white around the telephone receiver as she remembered Steve's account of the man who'd questioned him earlier that day. A man Steve had instinctively mistrusted. "How did you get this number? It's unlisted."

"One of your associates provided it to me. I'm sorry, I hope I'm not imposing too greatly on your time, but it really is very important that I get in touch with Ms. Gibson. It's in regard to a rather sizable inheritance. I'm sure she'll be very pleased to hear from me."

And if Casey bought that, he'd probably try to sell her some ocean-front property in Arizona. She didn't believe a word he'd just said. "I'm sorry, Mr. Park, was it?" she said, aware that he'd given Steve a different name. "Ms. Gibson left my employ without giving notice. She did the same thing to my competitor, Lockhart Air," she added, biting back a scathing, *As you already know.*

"Neither of you has heard from her since she quit?"

"No. And it was quite inconvenient for me—as it was for Mr. Lockhart. We neither know nor care where she is now."

"If you hear from her—"

"I won't. And please don't bother me again. Good day, sir." With that curt dismissal, she hung up the phone.

Only then did her knees weaken. "Oh, my God," she whispered.

Then she bolted for the door. She needed to talk to Steve.

5

STEVE OPENED THE DOOR moments after Casey rang his doorbell, just as she was about to press it again. Her thoughts were just clear enough for her to notice that he wasn't holding Annie. She reached out to clutch his arm, taking her first deep breath since she'd left her apartment after that weird phone call. "Is everything all right here?"

"Yes, fine. What's wrong? You look as though you've seen a ghost."

She didn't let go of his arm. She found comfort in the rock-solid strength of him—though she was reluctant to admit that, even to herself. "Where's Annie?" she asked, forcing her thoughts away from the warmth of Steve's arm beneath her hand.

"She's in the bassinet. I just fed her and rocked her to sleep. She probably won't stay down long, but—"

"He called me," Casey cut in. "At my house. My unlisted number."

Steve went still, his eyes narrowing. "Who called you?"

"Claybrook. The guy you told me about. Only he used another name this time."

He drew her into the house and shut the door behind her. Casey didn't pull away when he covered her hand with his. The contact was rather reassuring at the moment. "What did he say to you?" Steve asked.

"Almost the same words he used with you. He asked if Janice worked for me and if I know how to reach her. Only this time he mentioned an inheritance."

Steve frowned. "He didn't say anything about an inheritance to me."

"I didn't believe him, Steve. I hope I did the right thing—God knows Janice could use some financial help—but knowing what he'd said to you earlier made me certain he was lying."

"What did you say to him?"

"I told him that Janice had quit without notice. I insinuated that I was very annoyed with her for leaving me in the lurch, and that you were, too. I left it that I didn't know or care where Janice is now."

Steve smiled a little. "I'm sure you said it in that snotty, I'm-the-boss-don't-mess-with-me voice you do so well."

For once she didn't take offense at his teasing. "I tried."

He nodded. "I'd bet he bought it. He'd have no reason not to believe you."

"His voice was so creepy, it made me nervous. I hope he couldn't tell. How do you suppose he found my number?"

"These days, even an unlisted number isn't that

hard to find. Someone who's a bit too clever with a computer—or a bit too smooth with people who know it—can usually find what they want."

"He said he got it from one of my associates. I can't imagine anyone who works for me giving a stranger my number. But if he's been snooping around the airport, he probably knows how recently Janice disappeared. And that she was pregnant when she left."

Steve nodded. "You're right. But, Casey, he has no reason at all to think you and I have her baby. No one knows that except us, Madelyn and B.J. And neither of them will tell him. I've talked to both of them today and we've agreed to keep this quiet for now."

The whole situation was giving Casey an ulcer. She placed a hand on her aching stomach and wished she had an antacid handy. "What if there's some legitimate reason this guy's looking for Janice? What if she's really in line for an inheritance? Or maybe her family is looking for her—a family who could possibly help her now."

"Even if Claybrook does represent Janice's family, we've done nothing wrong. We haven't lied. We really *don't* know where she is now or how to reach her. And he hasn't asked about Annie."

His reassurances didn't loosen the knots in Casey's stomach. It was obvious to her that she and Steve were in over their heads. She was much more comfortable feuding with him over business issues than collaborating with him in a situation that could affect little Annie's entire life.

As if in response to her troublesome thoughts, Annie began to fuss, her cries carrying clearly from the bedroom. "I'll get her," Casey said, needing something productive to do. "There are several bags of baby supplies in the backseat of my car. Would you bring them in, please?"

Steve took her car keys from her hand and stepped outside. She headed for the bedroom. Annie was working herself into a full tantrum when Casey reached her, her tiny face red, her eyes squeezed shut, her fists and feet pumping. Casey slid her hands beneath the active little body and lifted the baby into her arms.

"I've always believed assertiveness was a good thing for a woman," she murmured, patting Annie's back, "but I think you're carrying it a little too far."

Annie burped noisily.

"Whatever works for you," Casey said with a faint smile.

She carried the hiccuping infant into the den where Steve was unloading bags. "Looks like you picked up everything we could ever need," he commented, examining a soft pink hairbrush.

"I thought we'd better try to give her a bath after dinner," she said. Then she gasped. "Dinner! I was going to bring takeout, but that creepy phone call knocked it right out of my head."

Steve smiled. "Don't sweat it. Why don't I run out

and pick something up while you give Annie her bottle?"

She returned his smile apologetically. "Sounds like a good plan."

"What would you like?"

"I'm not choosy tonight. Whatever sounds good to you will be fine with me."

His grin deepened. "Why do I get the feeling I'd better not get too accustomed to hearing you say things like that?"

She made a determined effort not to look at his dimples, so that she could keep her voice level and firm. "Bet on it."

His expression became more serious when he took a step closer to her. "I won't be gone long. You'll be okay?"

She knew he was remembering the way she'd looked when she'd arrived—shaken, wild-eyed, clinging to him—thoroughly unnerved by a mere telephone call. "I'll be fine, Steve. I was just a little rattled by the call because I wasn't expecting it."

"Yeah, well, he rattled me a little, too." He stroked the line of her jaw with his knuckles. "I'll be back soon."

He really was going to have to stop touching her that way, Casey thought as he walked out, closing the door behind him. It was growing increasingly difficult to think of him as an enemy when her whole body was tingling like crazy from a mere brush of his knuckles.

Annie made a sound that probably expressed hunger, but sounded to Casey almost like mocking amusement. Casey sighed. "You're right. I'm an idiot. Let's go find your dinner."

She started to relax once she'd settled in the big rocker in Steve's den with the baby in her arms, the only sound in the quiet room being the little slurping sounds Annie made. She cuddled the baby against her and Annie's blue eyes locked with hers. The child stopped nursing for a moment to study Casey more closely, and then she began to work the nipple again without looking away.

Funny how many times during the past twenty-four hours Casey had found herself imagining what it would be like if Annie were hers. She realized now that her maternal instincts had merely been suppressed during the past stressful year, not extinguished. There was something very sweet and touching about having this helpless, totally dependent child trust her so implicitly. Something that made her old longings for a family of her own resurface with a vengeance.

She touched Annie's palm and smiled when the baby's miniature fingers closed firmly around her own. It made her sad to think of how many of these precious moments Janice was missing.

"We'll find your mommy for you, sweetie," she murmured, hoping she wasn't making an empty promise.

She was a bit surprised when the doorbell rang a

few minutes later. Steve wouldn't have rung the bell...unless his hands were full and he couldn't unlock the door, she thought, hoping that was the explanation. Cradling Annie in her left arm, she walked to the door and peeked out the narrow security window.

It wasn't Steve, she realized immediately. But it wasn't anyone to fear, either.

She opened the door. "Hello, B.J."

His bushy red eyebrows rose. "Well, hey, Casey. Didn't expect to find you here consorting with the enemy."

"I'm only giving Steve a hand with the baby," she answered repressively. "He's gone out to pick up some dinner, but he should be back in a few minutes if you want to come in and wait."

She moved out of the way to allow the big man to amble past her, closing the door behind him. B.J. tentatively reached out with one thick finger to touch Annie's tiny hand. "How's the kid doing?"

"She makes sure she gets what she wants."

He chuckled. "Good for her. Considering who's been taking care of her, she's got to be able to fend for herself a bit."

"I'll have you know we've been taking very good care of her."

His grin was a bit wicked. "We?" he repeated. "Never thought I'd hear you linking yourself with Steve."

"It's only until we've settled this situation," she

muttered, glaring at him. She had always considered B.J. even more annoying than Steve—and that was saying a lot.

He sobered. "Heard anything from Janice since she called last night?"

Apparently, he had talked to Steve earlier. Casey shook her head. "Nothing. Have you found anything?"

"No. I've talked to everyone I can think of. She doesn't seem to have any friends around here. Her neighbors in the trailer park hardly ever saw her. She paid her rent in cash, since apparently she didn't have a bank account. It's like she just disappeared off the face of the earth. To tell you the truth, Casey, I'm beginning to think you were right. We should have called the police."

She chewed her lower lip a moment, glancing at the baby, who gazed so sweetly back up at her. "Maybe we should have," she agreed after a moment. "But it's harder now."

B.J. nodded, his expression just a bit surprised. Had he really thought her so callous? Was it possible that she had misjudged him as badly as he had her?

B.J. pushed his hands into his pockets, looking uncharacteristically grave. "Some guy came up to me at the airport a couple of hours ago, asking questions about Janice."

Casey's throat tightened. "What was his name?"

"Park. I forget the first name."

"Walter?"

B.J. nodded. "Yeah, that's it. Do you know him?"

"He called me at home earlier. Did you give him my number?"

Frowning, B.J. shook his head. "I don't have your number."

So she still didn't know where the guy had gotten it. "What did he say to you?"

"He asked if I knew Janice, if I'd heard from her lately. Asked if I had any suggestions for where he might find her."

"Did he tell you why he was looking for her?"

"Said something about working for her family. I didn't know whether to believe him or not, to be honest. Not after Steve told me how frightened Janice sounded when she called."

"I didn't believe him, either," Casey confessed.

"Man, this stinks. I don't like the thought that someone could be trying to hurt Janice. And I don't like not knowing how to help her...or the kid," he added, nodding toward Annie.

"Neither do I, B.J."

The front door suddenly opened, causing them both to whirl in that direction. Casey clutched Annie tightly to her chest.

Steve looked surprised when he walked in, carrying a large, aromatic bag. "Did I startle you guys?"

"A little. B.J. was just telling me that Park contacted him this afternoon."

Frowning, Steve looked at his pilot. "He called himself Park?"

B.J. nodded. "Walter Park. Smooth-looking guy with gray hair and hard eyes. Grilled me about whether I knew where Janice was, asked if I thought there was any chance you or Casey would know. I told him none of us know where she is. Guess he could tell I was telling the truth, because he didn't hang around long."

"Did he ask about the baby?" Casey asked, cradling Annie protectively.

B.J. shook his head. "Not a word."

Steve frowned. "You said he had gray hair?"

"Yeah."

"The guy who found me this morning had oily black hair. Rough skin, thick neck, a nose that looked like it had been broken a time or two."

His eyes wide, B.J. shook his head. "Not the same guy. This one looked like a banker or something. Thin, sharp dresser. Respectable, really. But I didn't like his eyes."

Casey sank into the rocking chair, her knees going suddenly weak. "There are two of them?"

"Apparently."

"You suppose they're working for the same people?" B.J. asked.

Steve shrugged, looking worried. "I don't have a clue. For all we know, they could both be decent guys with Janice's best interests at heart...but I don't think so. Not after hearing the fear in her voice when she called here last night."

"Damn. I think I'll check on Madelyn and make

sure no one's been bothering her." B.J. moved toward the door. "Let me know if anything else comes up."

"We're about to have dinner. There's plenty of food for the three of us," Steve offered.

B.J. shook his head. "Thanks, but I'll grab something later. I'll be in touch."

He left without further comment.

"He is a very odd man," Casey commented, looking at the closed door.

"He's a little eccentric, but he has a heart as big as Texas. How's Annie?"

"She's starting to look sleepy. Maybe she'll nap while we eat."

"I'll move the bassinet to the kitchen. Maybe she'll be content to be in there with us."

Casey nodded, trying to get hold of her emotions. But the revelation that Claybrook and Park were two separate men had definitely ruined her appetite.

A FEW MOMENTS LATER, Steve summoned her to the kitchen. "Everything's ready in here. Want to try putting her down?"

Very carefully, Casey carried Annie into the other room and laid her gently in the bassinet. To her relief, Annie didn't stir, but settled into the little bed with a sleepy sigh.

"You're getting pretty good at that," Steve commented, watching her. "Have you ever wanted kids of your own?"

"They're on my list of things to do when I have time," she replied, lightly, trying to discourage getting too personal with him.

"Right after putting me out of business, I suppose."

Even though she didn't find the comment particularly funny, since that was exactly what she intended to do, she couldn't help but laugh a little at his cheerful tone. "Somewhere after that," she agreed.

"I hope you like Chinese food."

Having recognized the bag he'd carried in, she nodded. "I love Chinese food. Especially when it's prepared by Sam Wing."

"Then you're in luck. Mr. Wing personally prepared our dinner this evening."

Having been unsure of her preferences, Steve had provided a variety of dishes. More than they could possibly eat, actually. He shrugged when she pointed that out. "I'll have leftovers for breakfast tomorrow," he said.

She wrinkled her nose at the thought of eating Chinese leftovers before noon. Then sighed in appreciation at the first bite of Kung Pao chicken. She supposed Mr. Wing's food was good enough to enjoy any time of day.

They ate in silence for a few minutes, both lost in their thoughts. And then Steve spoke, breaking into Casey's troubling reverie. "Tell me about yourself, Casey."

Surprised by the request, she studied him across the table. "What do you mean?"

He smiled faintly. "I thought it was fairly self-explanatory. I'd just like to get to know you better."

For the first time, Casey became fully aware that she and Steve were alone together in his home, if you didn't count Annie. Funny how it had taken her so long to find that circumstance so unsettling. Had she been too distracted to really notice before? Or was there suddenly something different in the way Steve was looking at her now? Something that made her aware of him as a man, rather than as a rival. "Why?"

He sighed. "Must you be so suspicious of everything I do or say? I'm simply trying to make conversation. We're both worried about Janice and Annie, but there's nothing we can do at the moment. We should at least attempt to enjoy our dinner."

She supposed she had overreacted a bit. It did seem silly for them to eat together in total silence. Her sudden discomfort at being alone with him was her problem, and she would deal with it. "Sorry. I guess I'm still on edge."

He nodded. "Perfectly natural after everything that's happened today. So why don't we talk about something else for a while?"

"What do you want to know?"

"Anything you want to tell me. Why don't we start with your job? Did you always want to take over your father's business?"

She shook her head, thinking that this was hardly a subject she should be discussing with Steve. And yet she found herself answering candidly. "Not exactly. I sort of fell into it when my father became ill a little more than a year ago. He and I ran JCS together the last few months of his life, and as you know, I took it over when he died last year."

"Your stepbrother wasn't interested in the business?"

"No. Edward's a dentist. That's all he wants to be."

"You said you didn't plan on taking over JCS. What *was* your plan?"

"I majored in accounting in college, because it seemed like a useful degree." One her father had recommended, of course, though she didn't bother to add that tidbit. "I spent five years earning a degree, and passed the CPA exam. I worked at that for a while, and then decided to go to law school." Another of her father's suggestions. "I was a little more than halfway through when Dad became ill."

Steve looked startled. "You quit law school?"

"My father needed me," she said simply, seeing no need to add that her heart hadn't really been in law, anyway.

Eating in silence for a moment, Steve studied her across the table until self-consciousness made her drop her gaze and concentrate on her own meal. "Why didn't you sell the business after your father died?" he asked eventually. "I know a lot of people expected you to do so."

"I couldn't. My grandfather started JCS. My father spent most of his life there. He asked me to keep it going..." That was only part of the reason she hadn't sold out, of course, but there was no way she was telling Steve Lockhart—her competition—the whole story.

"But if it isn't what *you* want—"

"I've learned to enjoy my work," she cut in a bit more sharply than she'd intended. "And I'm good at it, despite what some people predicted when I took over." The company accountant who had glumly forecast bankruptcy within a year, for example. Casey was still waiting to hear him admit that he had been wrong.

"I'm sure you would be good at whatever you choose to do. But still..."

She glared at him. "If you think I'd close my business so you can take over my clientele..."

His low, rich laughter sent a little shiver down her spine. "You are just about the most suspicious woman I've ever met. I'm only making conversation, not picking your brain in some subversive attempt to take over your business."

She refused to back down. Her chin rose even higher. "I wouldn't be surprised if you were."

"As I've mentioned before, I like you, too, Casey, darlin'."

He was the most annoying man. He simply loved

getting a rise out of her. And it always irritated her when she gave him that particular satisfaction. She took a deep breath and forced herself to speak calmly. "That's enough about me. What about you? Is this what you've always wanted to do?"

"Have dinner with you, you mean? Actually, it's been a goal of mine since the day we—"

"The charter service," she said through gritted teeth. "Have you always wanted to run your own charter service?"

"Oh, that." The glint in his brown eyes told her he had known exactly what she meant. "I've wanted to fly ever since I took my first plane ride when I was seven. It's all I ever wanted to do. I'm a bit too, um, independent to work for an airline—or for someone like you, for that matter—so I decided I'd better start my own company."

"Someone like me?" she repeated, her tone cool.

"Yeah. Someone with a thing for rules and procedures and longtime traditions."

"Rules and procedures are an important part of running a business. And there's nothing wrong with tradition."

He shrugged. "Anyway, I worked as a flight instructor in Dallas until I could convince a bank to risk giving me a business loan, which I managed two and a half years ago. And I've enjoyed every minute of it."

"Especially tormenting me, right?"

"Definitely one of the perks," he agreed with a flash of dimples.

"So what made you decide to start up here, as opposed to Dallas?"

"My father grew up in this area. We came to visit several times a year when I was growing up, and I always liked it here. Dallas has a surfeit of charter services, and the market seemed a bit more open here, so..." He allowed his voice to trail off.

Casey dabbed at the corners of her mouth with a paper napkin, glaring at him. "I think JCS was serving this area quite well before you came along."

"Have you got something against honest competition?" he asked mildly. "You aren't really advocating a monopoly, are you? Or suggesting JCS can't survive on its own merits?"

She opened her mouth to give him a blistering reply, but shut it again with a snap, reminding herself that he was only baiting her again. His decidedly warped sense of humor was going to get him in trouble someday. She would greatly enjoy being there to witness it, she thought darkly.

As though realizing she wasn't going to contribute any further to that particular debate, Steve changed the subject. "You don't have a pilot's license?"

Once again, he'd hit a nerve, touching on a criticism others had made, but Casey had always considered unfounded. "Being able to fly is not a prerequisite for managing a charter business. Just as a hospital administrator doesn't actually perform surgeries," she added.

"You never wanted to fly?" Steve persisted.

No way was she going to admit that she, the descendant of several generations of skilled pilots, was afraid to fly. She'd been in airplanes since she was born, and she'd never liked it. Her anxiety had increased as she got older, and by the time she was a teenager, she'd only go up when it was absolutely necessary.

Her father had all but demanded that she take flying lessons, believing she could conquer her fear if she became more familiar with the operation of an airplane. She had flatly refused. She would concentrate on schedules and spreadsheets, payroll and profits, she had announced, leaving the flying to others.

It was only one more time when she had disappointed her very demanding father.

"It never interested me," was all she said.

Steve might have pursued that topic further, but a small cry came from the bassinet. Steve peered in at the baby. "I think our peace and quiet is about to come to an end."

Annie opened her eyes, blinked a time or two, and then, realizing that she wasn't being held, let out an indignant squawk.

"You take care of her and I'll clean the kitchen," Casey offered.

"Deal." Steve stood and reached into the bassinet.

Relieved that the personal conversation was over for the time being, Casey turned her attention back to more pressing matters. She knew it was nearing the time when she should leave, but echoes of that eerie phone call kept playing through her mind. If Park, or whatever his name was, had found her unlisted number, he could find her home address just as easily. And what about this Claybrook character? Was he someone to worry about, as well?

"I thought newborns spent most of their time asleep," Steve said, holding Annie on his shoulder and patting her back as she bumped her wobbly head against him.

Casey closed the refrigerator and turned to him. "She does sleep a lot. She simply does it an hour or two at a time."

"I guess that's why it seems like she's awake so much."

"She was sleeping pretty heavily when we found her yesterday. She must have been exhausted." Casey thought about how warm it had been in the airplane and hoped Annie hadn't been affected. It couldn't have been good for her to be in that stuffy space for long. She wanted very badly to believe that Janice had been watching to make sure her baby was safe before deserting her.

Pushing those troubling thoughts to the back of her mind, she remembered one more thing she had planned to attempt this evening. "I suppose we should try giving her a bath while she's awake."

Steve gulped audibly. "Have you ever actually bathed a baby?"

"No. I don't suppose you..."

"Never. So, what's the plan? I assume she's too small for the bathtub."

She nodded. "The kitchen sink?" she suggested, motioning toward his deep, porcelain double sinks.

He considered it a moment, then nodded. "That'll probably work best this time."

He made it sound as though they'd be doing this often. Casey frowned. She wanted this situation settled soon—for the sake of everyone involved. They couldn't go on this way much longer.

She moved abruptly toward the doorway. "I'll go get the stuff I bought. I'll be right back."

"There are towels in the linen cabinet in the front bath," he called after her. Then in a low voice, he added, "You'd probably better bring several. This could get messy."

6

CASEY RETURNED to the kitchen with her arms loaded. She dropped everything on the counter and began to arrange it, trying to look as if she knew what she was doing. Spreading one thick, soft towel on the counter next to the sink, she then folded a thinner one and lined the bottom of one of the sinks with it. She hoped that would keep the baby from slipping on the cool, slick porcelain. After filling the sink with a couple of inches of warm water, she set the plastic bottle of baby soap nearby.

Laying another towel on the other side of the sink next to a diaper and clean sleeper, she drew a deep breath. "I guess we're ready," she said, turning to Steve.

"You could try saying that with a bit more confidence."

She smiled shakily. "I have to admit this makes me a bit nervous."

"Have you changed your mind?"

She shook her head. "Let's do it."

Steve laid Annie carefully on the first towel. And then he stood aside to let Casey remove the baby's sleeper and diaper. "Okay," she said, sensing that he was letting her take charge of this operation. "You set her in the sink and support her while I wash her. She's going to be slippery, so get a good hold."

Picking up the naked, wiggling baby, Steve murmured, "You aren't wearing a diaper at the moment, so show some respect for your elders, will you, kid?"

Annie made a gurgle that could have been interpreted as amusement, but was more likely just a coincidence. Once Steve had Annie in position, Casey dipped the little washcloth she'd bought into the warm, soapy water and moved in to begin washing.

Maybe their system wasn't the accepted method for baby-bathing, but it worked for them. Annie actually seemed to enjoy the experience, going very still as the washcloth stroked gently over her skin.

Casey had to stand quite close to Steve to reach the baby. Her attention was focused so much on Annie at first, she barely acknowledged Steve's proximity. And then she gradually began to notice the warmth that seemed to radiate from him. The way he loomed over her, making her aware of his size and strength. The way his big hands so securely cradled Annie's tiny body, making Casey unable to resist wondering how those hands would feel against her own bare back.

Stupid thought, she told herself, frowning and concentrating more intently on the task at hand. A likely result of stress, worry and overindulgence in Chinese food. And maybe a carryover from an unexpected kiss that had haunted her all afternoon.

"She likes this," Steve murmured.

Casey cleared her throat. "Yes, she certainly seems to. I was afraid she would scream."

"You should know by now that our Annie isn't predictable."

Our Annie. The casually-spoken phrase made Casey swallow again. It sounded just a bit too intimate for her peace of mind.

Steve shifted his weight, his shoulder and thigh brushing Casey as he moved. "Does it seem, um, warm in here to you?" she blurted, feeling heat creeping up to her cheeks.

"Oh, yeah," he murmured. "Getting warmer all the time."

She dropped the washcloth into the water with a splash. "I think she's clean enough now."

Steve's chuckle was obviously at her expense. But all he said was, "You want me to lay her on this other towel?"

She nodded. "Don't let her slide out of your hands."

One hand under the baby's neck, the other beneath her wet bottom, Steve transferred her with ease from the sink to the waiting towel, wrapping it around her and gently drying the busy little limbs. The tenderness with which he treated the baby brought an increasingly familiar lump to Casey's throat. She was spending entirely too much time with these two, she told herself. She was finding it more and more difficult to keep her distance from Steve Lockhart.

"You want to dress her?" Steve asked over his shoulder.

She nodded and moved to take his place at the counter.

"Would you like a cup of tea?"

"It's getting late," she answered, sliding a diaper beneath the baby's bottom. "I need to be going soon."

"You have time for one cup of tea," he said enticingly.

Carefully stuffing Annie's arms and legs into the sleeper, Casey conceded. "All right. Thank you."

When the sleeper was snugly fastened, she rubbed a dry corner of the towel over Annie's fuzz of damp, dark hair, then used the soft-bristled baby hairbrush to smooth the fine locks into place. "There you go, sweetie," she murmured, lifting the sweet-smelling baby into her arms and placing a kiss on Annie's satiny forehead. "All done."

Annie gurgled and stuffed her fist into her mouth. *Enough of this nonsense*, she seemed to say. *Where's the food?*

Grinning, Steve stuck a bottle into the microwave while he steeped the tea. "She wasn't about to let us have an evening snack without giving her one."

"You think we should be trying to keep her on some sort of regular feeding schedule? She doesn't seem to have a timetable when it comes to eating."

"Give her a break, Casey. She's so tiny, it's going to take a lot of formula to put some weight on those little bones. If she thinks she's hungry, then she probably is."

"I wonder what the child-care experts would think of that philosophy."

"Some of them would say it makes sense. Others would probably think I need a few years of analysis," he quipped with a grin.

"Something I always rather believed, myself," she murmured, making him laugh.

Steve managed to sip his tea while feeding the baby. But Casey found it hard to relax.

"You've gotten awfully serious. What's wrong?"

Steve's question made her realize that she'd been daydreaming, staring into her teacup. She blinked and made an effort to smile. "I guess I'm getting tired. It's been a long couple of days."

"You're probably looking forward to getting home."

"Yes, of course."

Apparently, she'd hesitated a moment too long before answering. His left eyebrow shot up. "You're not thinking about that telephone call again, are you?"

"It's crossed my mind a time or two."

"Are you afraid to go home?"

"Of course not. What a silly—"

"Because if you are," he cut in as if he hadn't heard her, "you're welcome to spend the night here.

You'd be doing me a favor, actually. We could take turns pacing the hallway with Her Highness."

She shook her head, refusing to be tempted by his offer. While there was a certain appeal in not going home alone this evening, she didn't want Steve to think she was a coward who couldn't take care of herself. She'd been living on her own for a long time. She didn't need a big, strong male to defend her against bumps in the night. Though it might have been nice, just this once, to know there was someone at her side...

She spoke firmly. "I don't need to stay overnight. And you don't really need me here. You managed just fine without me last night."

"I can manage," he agreed. "But if you're going to lose sleep worrying and I'm going to lose sleep pacing, we might as well lose sleep together, don't you think?"

"I'm not spending the night here, Steve."

"Not even if I promise to be on my best behavior? I won't tease you—much—and I won't kiss you again. Unless you want me to, of course."

The last comment reinforced her determination to leave. Of course she didn't want Steve to kiss her again, she told herself firmly. Not in her rational moments, anyway.

The fact that she occasionally experienced an irrational urge where Steve was concerned gave her even more reason to flee to the safety of her own apartment. "I'd really rather not. But I appreciate your offer. I'm sure you were only being thoughtful."

"Of course," he said, the twinkle in his eyes anything but selfless.

Now that she'd been bathed and fed, Annie drifted off to sleep again. Casey held her while Steve returned the bassinet to the bedroom, and then they stood side-by-side to put her to bed for the night—at least for the first shift of the night, Steve amended.

When Annie was settled, Steve walked Casey to the living room, where she retrieved her purse and shoes. "You're sure you won't change your mind about staying?" he asked.

"I'm sure," she said, her tone firm enough to convince both of them. Her fingers fumbled with the car keys—not a sign of reluctance to leave, she assured herself. Merely clumsiness.

"You aren't still worried about that phone call?"

She slung the strap of her purse over her shoulder. "You've persuaded me that there's nothing to worry about. As you said, there's no reason for the guy to contact me again."

"Oh. Well, I'm glad I was able to reassure you."

He didn't sound particularly glad, but she didn't call him on it. She moved to the front door with Steve right at her heels.

He reached out to place a hand against the door to prevent her from opening it. The unexpected move left her crowded between the door and his solid body. Once again she became aware of the warmth that seemed to radiate from him. Oddly enough, that masculine heat caused a slight shiver to course through her.

"Did—" She cleared her throat. "Did you forget something?"

"Yeah. I forgot to thank you again for everything you've done today."

She glanced up at him. "That isn't necessary."

"Oh, I think it is. Thank you, Casey, darlin'." He lowered his head and, before she could pull away, settled his mouth firmly on hers.

Just like the last time he'd kissed her, the first jolt of contact paralyzed her. The few times she had allowed herself to fantasize about kissing Steve Lockhart in the past, she'd assumed the experience would be merely intriguing.

Once again, she'd underestimated him.

It took her several long moments to pull away— probably because it took her that long to convince herself she really wanted to do so. Steve didn't try to detain her when she drew her head back, but he didn't move away, either. "You said you wouldn't do that again," she accused, her voice shaky. "You said you would be on your best behavior."

"That was if you spent the night," he reminded her with a quick smile. "Since you declined that offer..."

He lowered his head and kissed her again.

Maybe she could blame her lack of resistance on shock. She hadn't exactly cooperated, but she hadn't pushed him away, either. She didn't know what excuse she would use for not doing so this time.

His lips moved slowly, savoring hers, slanting to an angle that allowed him to taste and explore very thoroughly. It was only reflex that made her lips soften beneath his, she tried to convince herself. Only instinct that made her hands rise tentatively to clutch his shoulders. Only hormones that sent her blood coursing hotly through her, causing her skin to go warm and damp and her breath to catch hard in her throat.

Maybe it was only curiosity that kept her in his embrace a few heartbeats after her common sense kicked in and told her she had to put an end to this.

Her hands slid from his shoulders to his chest. Her fingers spread and pushed very lightly—but enough to get his attention. He lifted his head, the faint smile on his lips mirrored in his eyes. "I always knew kissing you would be spectacular," he murmured. "And, as I discovered earlier today, it is."

Had he really been so confident? Though the urge to kiss Steve had crossed Casey's mind a time or two, she had believed she'd be able to avoid the situation.

It seemed she'd been wrong about that, too.

Embarrassed already, she cleared her throat and tried to think of something to say.

What she *should* have said, of course, was that she didn't want it to happen again. Ever. That she had no intention of getting involved with him—if that was what he had in mind. She should have made it quite clear that once Annie and Janice were taken care of, the truce was over. She should have told him that no matter how good he looked or how fabulously he kissed, she couldn't let him distract her from the mission she'd undertaken when she'd left law school to rescue her father's business.

What she actually said was, "Um—it's getting late. I have to go."

To her relief—and unaccountable disappointment—he stepped back, putting a little distance between them. "Drive carefully," he said. "And call me when you're safely inside your apartment, will you?"

She looked at him blankly. "Why?"

"Because if you don't, I'll worry," he answered with a matter-of-fact shrug.

Even as she nodded and let herself out, she was aware that it had been a long time since anyone had worried about whether she got home safely.

CASEY HAD DRIVEN only a couple of miles toward her home when she realized that she was being followed.

She might not have noticed the vehicle at a discreet distance behind her had her nerves not been so on edge—from the call earlier *and* from Steve's kisses. But when she made two completely illogical turns and noticed that the car was still behind her, though at a distance apparently intended to allay suspicions, she knew it was no coincidence.

She snatched up her cell phone and dialed Steve's number—a number she'd memorized as easily as he had hers.

"Someone's following me," she blurted, barely giving him time to answer.

Steve didn't hesitate. "Come back here. I'll be waiting at the front door for you."

"Should I call the police?"

"And tell them about Annie? Not yet, Casey. Just get back here and we'll talk about what to do."

"I just headed in your direction," she said, glancing at the distant lights reflected in her rearview mirror.

"Stay on the phone until you get here."

She heard the baby crying in the background. "What's wrong with Annie?"

"The phone woke her. She wants me to pick her up."

Casey made a careful one-handed left turn. "Shouldn't you take care of her?"

"It won't hurt her to fuss for a few minutes. Stay on the line, Casey."

She didn't want to dwell on how natural it seemed to have turned to him. How reassuring it was to hear his deep, concerned voice. How implicitly she trusted him to help her. This wasn't the time to worry about the kisses they'd shared or whether it would be possible to go back to the adversarial relationship they'd maintained before they'd found Annie in his plane.

There were more pressing matters at hand, she reminded herself with another nervous glance at the mirror.

"Casey?"

"Still here," she assured him. "I just turned onto your street. I see your house now."

"Okay. I'm hanging up. I'll meet you outside."

He was waiting on the front porch when she turned into his driveway. Just the sight of him, so strong and solid looking in the soft yellow glow of the porch lights, made the tense muscles in her neck relax a little.

She would worry about that reaction later, she decided, choosing for now to just be glad he was there.

Before the trailing vehicle had even reached Steve's driveway, Casey was out of her car and on his porch. He reached out to pull her close to him and together they watched the other car slow. Casey felt Steve's arm tense, and knew he was mentally preparing for trouble. She could feel the anger in him, and she suspected it was because she had been frightened.

The car suddenly sped away, disappearing into the night.

"Did you get the license plate number?" Steve asked, squinting after the nondescript dark vehicle.

She shook her head as the first tremor ran through her. "No."

His arm tightened around her. "Let's get inside."

Moving almost robotically, Casey went straight to

the wailing baby and lifted her out of the bassinet. She didn't know if she was offering comfort or seeking it, but it seemed to work both ways. Annie stopped crying. Casey snuggled the baby into her shoulder, resting her cheek against her soft little head.

As concerned as she was about whatever they'd stumbled into, she knew one thing for sure—there was no way she could hand this baby over to strangers now.

Steve was frowning and pacing the living room when Casey carried Annie in. "Okay," he said, turning to Casey as if in sudden decision. "I'm going to try again to reach Blake—the P.I. I mentioned to you before. I haven't been able to find him so far. He was still in Texas last I heard, but that was a while ago and he moves around a lot. There are a couple of people I can call who might know how to reach him."

"You think he'll know what we should do?"

Looking rueful, Steve shrugged. "He has to have a better idea than I do. He's the P.I.—I'm just a pilot."

A pilot who was going to an awful lot of trouble for a baby that wasn't his, Casey added silently. A pilot who had been prepared to face down the person who'd followed Casey and scared her half-silly. A pilot who had made her feel safe and protected just by standing beside her on his front porch.

It wasn't going to be easy to go back to comfortably hating him when this was all over, she thought.

Not that she was the kind of woman who wanted a man's protection, she reminded herself impatiently. "So what do we do now?"

"I'll make a couple of calls while you try to get Annie back to sleep. You can take the spare bedroom tonight. Annie can stay in the bassinet in my room."

Casey still wasn't comfortable with the prospect of spending the night here, but she was even less enthused about the idea of returning home alone when whoever had been following her might be waiting for her there. "I'll stay," she said. "But remember what you promised me earlier."

A quick flash of a wicked grin momentarily lightened his somber expression. "I'll behave—for as long as you want me to."

"I think we both know the answer to that," she said primly.

When he suddenly laughed, she realized he hadn't taken her words exactly as she'd intended them. "A guy can only hope, Casey, darlin'."

AN HOUR LATER, Annie had been fed again and was sleeping in the bassinet. "Maybe this time she'll stay asleep for a while," Steve said in a low voice, leading Casey out of the room.

"She's too young to sleep through the night, I suppose."

He nodded. "I set out some things for you in the spare bedroom. If you need anything else, don't hesitate to let me know."

He couldn't quite read her expression. "I'm sure I'll be fine," she answered. "Thank you."

Pausing outside the door to the spare bedroom, he reached out to brush a strand of hair away from her face. She looked pale, he thought. Tired. Yet still beautiful. "Everything will be all right, Casey."

"I'm afraid we've gotten in over our heads," she admitted. "We don't know who's looking for Janice or why someone was following me tonight. We don't know where Janice is, what she's running from, how she'll be able to take care of her baby when—or if— she comes back. I'm afraid we should have called the police immediately after we found Annie—for the sake of everyone involved."

"We can call them right now if you feel that's what you have to do," Steve said steadily, though it wasn't easy for him to make the offer. Still, Casey was as involved with this as he was. She was the one who'd been followed and was now so frightened she didn't want to go home. If she wanted to turn this problem over to the police, he could hardly blame her—even though the last thing he wanted was to get the bureaucrats involved.

He never had been one to let others deal with his problems, he thought.

Casey hesitated long enough to make him nervous, then shook her head. "I can't call them now," she admitted, glancing toward his bedroom where Annie slept. "I can't just give the baby to strangers without knowing why Janice left her with us—with you, anyway."

Relieved, Steve nodded. "We'll give it another day. Let's see what Blake says, if I can locate him. Or maybe Janice will call again."

"And if Claybrook or Park contacts us again?"

"I hope they do," Steve muttered, his fingers twitching with the urge to make the jerk pay for frightening Casey. "I've got a few things I'd like to say to whoever followed you tonight."

Casey swallowed nervously. "I just wish we knew what they want."

"We'll find out," he promised rashly. "We'll get through this, Casey. Together."

Her eyes widened a little at that, and he knew it was because she was more accustomed to thinking of him as a rival than as a partner. As much as he'd enjoyed their former sparring, he much preferred having her on his side.

"Is there anything I can do for you tonight?" he asked, reluctant to step away from her.

She shook her head. "No, thank you."

"You'll let me know if you need anything?"

"I'm sure I'll be fine."

His gaze drifted down to her mouth, which looked soft and vulnerable without the carefully-applied lipstick she wore at work. He remembered exactly how she tasted—and he hungered for another sample. He was tempted to capture that lovely mouth with his—but he had promised to behave if she stayed the night. Which didn't mean he couldn't ask...

He touched a fingertip to her lower lip. "Would I be totally out of line if I ask for a good-night kiss?"

Her lip quivered beneath his touch. Her cheeks grew pink, and her eyelids dropped to hide her expression from him. "I really don't think that's a good idea."

Looking at her mouth, he murmured, "It sounds like a damned good idea to me."

"Steve..."

He sighed regretfully. "I know. I promised. But it was definitely worth a shot."

She glanced up at him and he wondered if he caught a fleeting glimpse of temptation in her expression. Probably just wishful thinking, he decided when she reached behind her, opened the door and stepped backward into the bedroom. "Good night, Steve," she said, closing the door neatly in his face.

"Good night, Casey, darlin'," he murmured to the unresponsive wood.

He had her in his house, he thought as he moved toward his own room. Not quite in the way he had in mind—but it was certainly a step in the right direction.

CASEY SAGGED against the bedroom door for several long moments, telling herself she hadn't really just been tempted to grab Steve Lockhart and kiss him senseless. It had only been a crazy, fleeting impulse—probably the result of a confusing, stressful day. There'd been no chance that she would actually follow up on it, of course.

Her gaze fell on the neatly turned-down bed and her mind filled with images of other impulses she had no intention of pursuing with Steve.

Telling herself she needed a brisk slap in the face to bring her to her senses, she ran her hands through her hair and moved toward the bed. Steve had been very thoughtful, she noted. A large black T-shirt lay beside a pair of soft black sweatpants. A fluffy towel and washcloth had been laid beside the garments. There was even a new toothbrush, still in the package, and an unopened tube of toothpaste.

Her mouth quirked into a reluctant smile when she spotted the wrapped chocolate candy on her pillow.

He really was a nut, she thought, picking up the candy and cradling it in her hand. If their circumstances were different...if she didn't feel that she still had so much to prove...if she thought there was even a remote chance that two people so very different could have a relationship that didn't end in total disaster...

She shook her head, telling herself there was no reason to waste time on foolish daydreams when she had so many other things on her mind.

Still, she couldn't stop herself from vividly remembering Steve's kisses as she dressed for bed.

7

THE LIGHTED DIAL of her watch read 2:00 a.m. when Casey awakened to the sound of a baby crying. Disoriented for a moment, she wondered if she'd fallen asleep with the television on again...and then she remembered exactly where she was. And why.

She heard the deep rumble of Steve's voice as he passed her door, obviously carrying the baby whose howls had subsided to whimpers. Casey couldn't hear what he was saying, but she suspected he was trying to soothe the baby so Casey wouldn't be disturbed. He would be headed for the kitchen and the bottles of formula he'd left waiting in the refrigerator. Handling it on his own, she thought, rolling onto her back and staring at the shadowed ceiling. Taking complete responsibility for little Annie's care.

He really was a most unusual man.

Knowing he had everything under control, she told herself to go back to sleep. It took nearly twenty minutes before she finally conceded that wasn't going to happen. With a sigh, she tossed off the covers and swung her bare feet to the floor. A glance downward assured her she was decent. Steve's black T-shirt swallowed her to her knees. Below that, the sweatpants she'd cinched tightly around her waist bagged around her ankles.

Wearing Steve's clothes, she thought. Sleeping in his spare bedroom. Caring for a baby with him.

She never would have dreamed when she'd chased him into his office yesterday to yell at him for stealing her customers that less than forty-eight hours later she would find herself in *this* situation.

He was sitting in the kitchen when she found him. He'd tossed a dish towel over his bare left shoulder and was supporting Annie against it, gently patting her back with his right hand. An empty baby bottle sat on the table in front of him, next to a nearly full glass of orange juice. He smiled at Casey when he spotted her in the doorway. "I'm sorry, did we disturb you?"

"No." Quickly averting her eyes from his bare chest—oh, God, he looked even better beneath his clothes than she'd fantasized!—she seized on the first excuse that came to her mind. "I'm thirsty," she said, moving toward the sink.

"There are milk and juices in the fridge."

"Tap water's fine," she replied, filling a glass.

A hollow burp from behind her let her know Steve had been successful. Sipping her water, she turned to face him again, somewhat prepared this time for the sight of him. He'd pulled on a pair of jeans, leaving his feet bare. His hair was tousled sexily around his face and there was a shadow of a beard on his jaw. His eyelids were heavy and his brown eyes gleamed softly as he studied her in return. She doubted that he missed one detail of her disheveled appearance, and self-consciousness made her hand a bit unsteady when she placed her empty glass in the dishwasher.

"Anyone ever tell you how fetching you look in the middle of the night, Casey, darlin'?"

His tone was low, intimate, blatantly enticing. She tried to glare at him, but knew her effort wasn't as effective as she might have liked. "Don't start that."

"Sorry. It just slipped out before I could stop it."

He wasn't at all sorry, of course. He'd known exactly what he was saying—and probably what it would do to her. She pointedly ignored him and looked at the baby. "She's still awake," she said unnecessarily.

Steve glanced automatically down at Annie, who lay in his arms looking around with wide eyes. "Of course she's awake. Her Highness follows her own schedule."

Annie made a sound that was a cross between a coo and a gurgle, and then looked surprised that the noise had emerged from her. Laughing softly, Steve leaned over her, murmuring nonsense and making faces while the baby watched him in fascination. Casey couldn't resist stepping closer, standing next to Steve as she enjoyed the funny expressions crossing Annie's little face. She bent closer, bringing her own face within Annie's line of vision, smiling when the baby spotted her and focused fiercely.

"Hello, sweetie," she crooned, reaching out to stroke the baby's impossibly soft cheek. "You look awfully smug and satisfied."

"Why shouldn't she be smug and satisfied?" Steve asked with a chuckle. "She has both of us hovering over her, ready to cater to her every whim. Got us both wrapped around her tiny little finger."

"But she doesn't have her mommy," Casey murmured, her mood turning melancholy as she found herself wondering where Janice was at that moment. Whether anyone was taking care of *her*.

"We're working on that," Steve said firmly. "As soon as I hear from Blake, we're going to start an all-out search for her. Even if it means getting the police involved."

"You really don't want to turn to the police, do you?"

"I have nothing against the police on the whole," he answered, his tone guarded. "It's the child welfare system that concerns me. I had a friend who grew up in the foster care system. Maybe it works most of the time, but some of the stories he told me would cause nightmares. I don't like the thought of Annie getting sucked into that."

"Neither do I, now that I've spent time with her," Casey admitted, gazing protectively at the helpless child. "I just hope it won't become necessary."

Suddenly aware that she'd subconsciously rested a hand on Steve's shoulder for balance—or had it been entirely subconscious?—she lifted her hand

and stepped aside. Her fingers curled into her palm, still tingling from the contact with his warm, bare skin. She noticed that Annie was starting to look a bit sleepy as Steve rocked her in his arms. "Looks like she'll be out again soon."

He nodded, answering quietly. "I hope so. We can all use some more sleep."

Watching the practiced rocking motions he made, she leaned against the counter, crossing her arms over her chest. "Are you sure you haven't had any experience with babies? You've certainly handled Annie like an old pro."

He smiled. "I did a bit of baby-sitting for my younger sister and brother, but nothing since."

"Are you close to your brother and sister?"

"Considering we're only able to get together a couple of times a year, we're pretty close, I suppose. You were an only child, weren't you?"

"Except for Edward, my stepbrother. My mother died when I was very young and my father married Edward's mother when I was six and Edward was ten."

"Is your stepmother still living?"

"No. I guess that's why Edward and I make an effort to stay in touch. We're the only family either of us has left, even though there's no actual blood connection."

"Were you close to your father?"

Steve had met Casey's father several times, of course, which probably explained the carefully neutral tone of his question. Casey knew her father had been openly hostile to the young man who'd had the audacity to go into direct competition with the long-established JCS. As she, herself, had been, she thought with a touch of discomfort. She couldn't blame Steve if he had disliked Louis Jansen. But she'd never known why her own prickliness toward Steve had always seemed to amuse him more than it annoyed him.

She phrased her answer with care, family loyalty urging her to be cautious about what she revealed. "My father and I got along well enough."

As long as she'd done everything her father wanted her to do, she could have added, but didn't, of course.

"From what I saw of him, he was rather...demanding. I don't expect he was an easy man to please."

"No, not easy," she admitted. "But he expected no more of others than he did of himself."

"Did he push you into leaving law school and taking over JCS?"

"Just the opposite, actually. He was afraid I couldn't handle it. But Edward didn't want it and Dad never found anyone else he trusted, so he had to turn it over to me and hope for the best." If her lingering resentment of her father's lack of faith crept into her voice, it wasn't intentional, but unavoidable.

Steve studied her expression. "You're still trying

to prove to him that he was wrong about you—even though he's been dead for a year."

She shrugged. "Maybe I just need to prove it to myself."

"Casey..."

"The baby's asleep," she said, unwilling to carry that particular topic any further. "Would you like me to carry her to bed while you finish your juice?"

He agreed, and Casey bent over to lift Annie carefully from his arms. Vividly aware of him, she concentrated intently on the baby. It was probably sleep deprivation that caused her to have the crazy urge to rest her cheek against his broad, bare shoulder, she told herself with exasperation. She should have gone home and faced the guy who'd followed her, rather than stay here and face her own weaknesses where Steve Lockhart was involved.

To her relief, Annie didn't wake up when Casey laid her in the bassinet. While she waited to make sure the baby was really asleep, Casey couldn't help noticing Steve's big bed, the tumbled covers giving evidence that he had scrambled out of it when Annie had demanded her bottle. The room was dark except for the small, dimmed lamp on the nightstand, casting the corners into deep shadows, giving the room an air of intimacy.

Forcing her eyes away from the bed, she turned firmly toward the doorway...only to find Steve standing there, watching her.

She pulled her gaze quickly away from his sleek bare chest and swallowed hard.

She really should have gone home.

"She's still asleep," she whispered, motioning toward the bassinet. "I guess we'd better try to get some rest ourselves while we can."

He didn't step aside when she moved toward the door. She hesitated a foot away from him. "You'll have to move so I can get by," she reminded him, nodding toward the doorway he filled so thoroughly.

"Yes, I know." But he remained where he was.

She slid her suddenly damp palms down her sides. "Steve?"

"Do you have any idea how hard it is for me to have you here like this and not touch you?" His tone was casual, almost conversational, in contrast to the words he'd spoken.

Casey's breath quivered. "Don't say that."

"Why not? It's true. Do you know how long I've fantasized about seeing you here, in my bedroom? How many months it's been since I've been out to dinner with another woman, because no one else fascinates me the way you do?"

She couldn't believe the things he was saying to her. He had flirted with her for months, but she'd always thought he was teasing her, baiting her. Was she supposed to believe that he had been seriously interested in her—and only in her?

"Steve, we—"

"Do you remember the first time we met?"

She remembered. It had been her first day on the job at JCS. Her father had just gotten out of the hospital and they had known even then that his time was limited. Already grounded from the flying he'd loved so much, he'd intended to teach Casey the business, preparing her to keep his cherished operation intact. He'd made no pretense of optimism.

"You'll probably have to declare bankruptcy within the first year," blunt-spoken Louis Jansen had muttered. "And there's the guy who'll put you under," he'd added, nodding toward the good-looking man who'd approached them from across the parking lot.

"Who is he?" Casey had asked, holding on to her strained patience with her father by reminding herself repeatedly that he was gravely ill.

"His name is Lockhart. He opened a cut-rate charter operation last year—you've probably heard me mention it."

She had, of course—in terms she couldn't have repeated in polite company.

"He's gunning for us," Louis had warned. "He wants to put us out of business. Smart-ass young punk has no respect for tradition."

Because it had been obvious that Steve Lockhart had been causing her father concern, Casey had been prepared from the start to dislike him. When he'd flashed her a brazen smile and given her an obviously approving once-over, she had reacted with a quiver of purely feminine response that had only infuriated her.

"New employee, Mr. Jansen?" Steve had asked her father, his courteous tone sounding a bit mocking to Casey's biased ears.

"My daughter, Casey," Louis had growled in response. "She's taking over my company while I take some time off later this year. And she's one damned sharp cookie, so don't think you'll make any more headway against her than you have against me, you hear?"

Even though she knew her father's words were mostly bravado, that he probably didn't even believe them, himself, Casey had treasured them. Compliments from her father had been so rare that she'd been willing to take them, regardless of the motivation behind them.

Steve had looked again at Casey, smiled in a way that had made her toes curl, and murmured, "I'll certainly look forward to trying."

"He'll win," Louis had predicted when Steve sauntered away. "He's hungry and willing to do whatever it takes to succeed. It'll be because of him that there will be no Jansen Charter Service at the airport for the first time in three generations. I always hoped I'd have a son to carry on the name. If I'd had a son like Steve Lockhart..."

Realizing that he'd been rambling aloud, he'd had the grace to look somewhat apologetically at Casey. "Not that you haven't been a good daughter," he'd assured her gruffly. "Never caused me any trouble. Not your fault that flying isn't in your blood the way it was in mine and your grandfather's."

It hadn't been the words he'd used that had caused Casey the most pain. It had been the reluctant admiration in his voice when he'd talked about the man he expected to put his daughter out of business. Knowing that her father would rather have his competitor for a son than Casey for a daughter had only made her more inclined to dislike Steve.

"Maybe flying isn't my thing, but business is," Casey had reminded Louis firmly. "JCS isn't dead, Dad. And Steve Lockhart is going to find that it takes more than a cocky grin and a pilot's license to outwit me."

The very faint gleam of approval in her father's eyes had been all the incentive she'd needed.

Later that day, she'd gotten her first look at the JCS financial records. And she'd realized that her father's failing health had affected him more than physically. She had never let him know how close he had come to destroying the company to which he had devoted so much of his life, how disastrous the decisions were that he'd made during the months before his illness had been diagnosed. He'd never understood what it had taken for her to put the company back on somewhat secure footing.

It hadn't helped that Lockhart Air had continued to flourish during the eighteen months since her first day on the job. The day her father had introduced her to Steve Lockhart.

"I remember the day we met," she murmured, forcing her thoughts back to the present.

"I wanted you then," Steve told her. "I took one look at you, standing there so overwhelmed, yet so determined, and I felt my knees go weak. Seeing you here, tonight, in my bedroom—it's all I can do to stand upright," he confessed with a slightly sheepish smile.

Her own legs trembled. She put out a hand to steady herself against one corner of his dresser. "You said you wouldn't do this."

"I haven't touched you. And I won't—unless you want me to. I just couldn't keep quiet any longer about the way I feel when I'm with you. I'm sorry if it makes you uncomfortable."

Uncomfortable? She might have laughed if she hadn't been so painfully close to panic. "Uncomfortable" was such an innocuous term compared to the tumultuous feelings he had evoked in her. "We should get some sleep," she blurted, seeking escape.

As if she would be able to sleep a wink now.

Steve nodded and moved aside, clearing the doorway so she could step through.

She was very careful not to look at him, not to touch him when she passed by. She wasn't tempted to stay, she assured herself, aware that he watched her as she walked rather stiffly toward the spare bedroom. Physical desire wasn't enough justification to throw away months of single-minded hard work.

She paused outside the door to the other bedroom, her gaze meeting Steve's over her shoulder. His eyes were steady as they met hers, his expression warm, sincere. She swallowed, feeling the need to say something. "Steve?"

"Yes?"

"I don't think I can deal with this now. Not with everything else that's going on."

"I won't press you. I've said my piece. The next move is yours, Casey."

There was only one logical move she could make, of course. She stepped into the spare bedroom and closed the door behind her. And then she sat on the side of the bed and buried her face in her trembling hands, wondering if her life would ever be the same again.

ANNIE SLEPT THE REST of the night. She was probably the only one of them who did, Casey thought wearily as she climbed out from her tangled bedcovers.

It was just after 6:00 a.m. She'd been awakened by the sound of Annie crying in Steve's room. As he'd done the night before, Steve carried the baby past Casey's door toward the kitchen, talking in the low, soothing voice he always used with Annie.

There was no question of trying to sleep any longer, of course. As tired as she was, Casey knew she would only lie in bed—as she had for the past three hours or so—hearing the echo of Steve's voice in her head. *Do you know how long I've fantasized about seeing you here, in my bedroom?*

Coffee, she thought, running both hands through her hair. She needed coffee. Gallons of it. Craving the caffeine more than she dreaded facing Steve again, she headed for the kitchen.

"Good morning." Sitting in the same chair she'd found him in during the night, Steve looked up from the baby in his arms. His easy smile didn't quite dispel the flare of heat in his eyes when he saw her.

"Good morning." She turned her own gaze quickly toward the coffeemaker on the counter. "I was going to make coffee, but I see you've already taken care of that."

"I set the timer last night. I figured Annie would be up by six. Looks like it's about ready."

Casey was already reaching into a cabinet for mugs. "Black, no sugar, right?"

"Right."

She poured two cups and set his in front of him, a safe distance away from the baby. "Would you like some breakfast?"

"Thanks, but I'm not really hungry yet. Feel free to help yourself to whatever you want, though."

She shook her head and sipped her coffee. "I don't usually eat this early, either."

"Something else we have in common."

She lifted her mug to her lips again for a careful sip that gave her an excuse not to respond.

For the next few minutes, the only sounds in the kitchen were the ones Annie made with her bottle, punctuated by the occasional burp Steve coaxed out of her. He was getting very good at this, Casey mused, noting how confident he'd become at handling the baby. More confident than Casey felt.

"What's our plan for today?" she asked, needing to distract herself from the way she felt watching him hold the baby so tenderly.

"I'm going to put in a few more calls to Blake. And I'm hoping Janice will call again to check on Annie. Maybe she'll give me a chance to convince her to come here and let us help her."

"And if she doesn't call today?"

A flash of frustration crossed Steve's face. "I don't know," he admitted. "Obviously, we can't keep on this way. We both have to get back to work. And every day that goes by is another day of uncertainty for Annie. She's starting to bond with us. She needs to be settled in a permanent home—preferably with her mother."

Casey nodded. "Surely Janice will call today. She has to know what she's asked of us—of you," she corrected herself. "She has to understand how difficult this has been for you."

"You're the one who has really been inconvenienced. You spent all day yesterday baby-sitting while I worked and then you couldn't even feel comfortable going home last night because some jerk tried to follow you."

"Do you think he believed I might lead him to Janice?"

"I can't imagine why else he would have followed you." Steve's dark frown let her know he hadn't taken the disturbing incident lightly.

Casey dragged both hands through her tousled hair. "I wish we knew what's going on. Why Janice is hiding. Why someone is so anxious to find her that he's been watching us. Whether we're making a terrible mistake by not calling the authorities."

From Steve's shoulder, Annie squeaked as if in protest. Steve's faint smile was ironic. "I guess she made her feelings clear about that."

Casey couldn't return the smile. She was too overwhelmed with everything that had happened during the past two days. Including the tension that was building between her and Steve.

Do you know how long I've fantasized about seeing you here, in my bedroom?

She set her empty coffee mug down with a thud. "I'd like to take a shower now, if you don't mind."

"Of course I don't mind," he chided her. "I'm only sorry you don't have any of your own things here."

She nodded. "I should probably go to my apartment after I've showered and dressed. Whoever followed me last night probably won't be as bold in the daytime."

"I'm still not comfortable with you going home alone yet."

"We shouldn't take the baby out. We don't want

whoever is looking for Janice to know we have her baby here."

Steve nodded. "I thought I'd call B.J. He's useless as a baby-sitter, but I bet he'd be happy to escort you to your place to get some of your things. I can't imagine anyone would bother you with B.J. at your side."

Thinking of B.J.'s massive proportions, Casey tended to agree. Still, she didn't like the implication that she needed a man beside her. She'd spent the past year learning to stand on her own feet, to emerge from behind her father's forceful shadow for the first time in her life.

"I don't think it will be necessary to call B.J.," she said firmly. "I let myself get rattled last night, but I'm fine now. If Park, or Claybrook, or whoever it was that followed me thinks he can intimidate me into telling him where Janice is—even if I knew—he's going to find himself in for a surprise. I'd love the chance to tell him exactly what I think about the sleazy, cowardly way he operates."

Steve chuckled. "I'm sure you would. And I bet his hair would be singed by the time you finish with him. But I'd still like to call B.J. Until we know exactly what we've gotten ourselves into, I'd rather not take any chances."

Annoyed by his paternalistic tone, she shook her head. "It's my chance to take. And *I'll* decide whether I want an escort or not. I don't need you to make arrangements for me."

Before he could argue further, she stood abruptly. "I'm going to take a shower."

Steve didn't try to stop her.

8

FORTY MINUTES LATER, Casey had cooled down enough to regret the sharp tone she had taken with Steve. He had only been concerned about her safety, she reminded herself. After the way she'd practically fallen apart last night, she could hardly blame him for thinking she needed his protection today. He'd only been concerned about her safety and peace of mind, and she'd reacted to his consideration by throwing the gesture back in his face.

She'd been prickly and defensive and belligerent toward him since the first day they'd met, she thought, chewing her lower lip. How could he be attracted to her?

Having toweled her long hair as dry as she could, she wrapped herself in the oversized terry cloth robe Steve had provided for her use—yet another thoughtful gesture on his part, she thought guiltily—and reached for the bathroom doorknob. She would have to wear the same clothes she'd had on yesterday, of course. She didn't like this feeling of being without her own things around her. She didn't like feeling so totally out of control.

Opening the bathroom doorway, she stepped into the hall and nearly plowed right into Steve.

He reached out to steady her when she would have stumbled. "Are you okay?"

"Yes, fine. Where's Annie?"

"Sound asleep. I moved the bassinet into the living room to give her a change of scenery while I cleaned the kitchen, and she dropped right off. I guess now that we're both wide awake, she decided to take a little nap," he added with a smile.

Casey realized suddenly that his hands were still resting on her shoulders. She was aware again that he wore nothing but a pair of jeans and that she wore only his bathrobe. That her skin was still flushed and moist from the shower and almost painfully sensitized to his touch. "I, um—I'd better get dressed."

"Don't go to all that trouble on my account," he murmured, brushing a strand of damp hair from her cheek with his thumb.

She shivered a little in response to the tender gesture. "Steve..."

"Are you cold?"

"No." Just the opposite, in fact. Heat was swirling through her in bone-melting waves, centering somewhere deep inside her. "But..."

His mouth was only inches from hers. "How can you look so beautiful this morning when you've barely slept a wink? Don't you know how unfair that is?"

Did he really think she was beautiful? She gave in

to a moment of pleasure at the compliment before making another attempt to be strong. "Steve, this—"

"I know my timing is lousy," he cut in ruefully. "And I know you wish I would just shut up and leave you alone. But, damn it, Casey, I'm only human. And I've dreamed of this for so very long."

He smothered her mouth beneath his before she could tell him that she did not want him to kiss her. And the lie evaporated from her mind, leaving only the stark truth behind. She wanted this kiss more than she wanted her next breath. She had been deluding herself, trying to believe otherwise.

Apparently she hadn't fooled Steve.

With a little moan of mingled misgiving, desire and surrender, she lifted her arms around his neck and returned the kiss with a hunger that equaled his. She wasn't kissing her business competitor this time, she thought dimly. Not the man who had taunted her and teased her and boldly stolen her customers. This kiss was for the man whose loyalty to his friends and employees surpassed his concern for his own well-being. The bachelor who had walked his floors with a tiny homeless baby. A man who was willing to risk so much just because a frightened young woman had asked for his help.

It had been hard enough to resist Steve when she'd convinced herself that she didn't like him. But now, after spending two days taking care of Annie with him, she could no longer pretend that she was immune.

He wasn't the only one who'd had fantasies since they'd met.

Emboldened by her response, he pulled her closer, his hands sliding from her shoulders down her back to settle at her hips. His mouth softened and the kiss changed from challenging to enticing.

Her lips parted, implicitly inviting him deeper. If she was going to throw away all caution, she might as well make it worth the risk, she figured. And when Steve claimed her mouth with a thoroughness that sent shock waves rippling all the way to her toes, she knew it was well worth whatever chance she was taking.

He lifted his hands, thrust his fingers into her hair and cupped her face between his palms. "Casey," he murmured, nibbling at her lips. "You'd better tell me to stop."

His hands weren't quite steady, she realized in wonder. He wanted her so badly it made him tremble. Could he possibly seduce her more completely?

"I don't think I can," she whispered.

He kissed her again—lightly, then more lingeringly, then almost roughly. "Casey," he muttered between kisses. "Darlin', if you want me to go away, now's the time to say so."

But she didn't want him to go away. She wanted him to keep kissing her. She wanted to feel those big, clever hands on her body. She wanted to discover for herself if the rest of him tasted as spicy and delectable as his mouth. She wanted to know how it felt to fly with him without ever leaving the ground.

She wanted Steve. And maybe, just this once, it was time for her to do something just for herself. Just once, she didn't want to be sensible and responsible and predictable, she thought, bringing her mouth to his again. It was time to make a choice based on her own desires, not a decision tailored to please someone else.

Just this once...

"Have you really dreamed about me, Steve?" she asked, her voice sounding unusually sultry even to her.

"Oh, yeah," he muttered, his lips moving against her cheek. "Too many times to count."

She ran her hands lingeringly across his bare shoulders, noticing again that his skin seemed unusually warm. It was almost as if the sheer masculine energy of him could hardly be contained. "Why don't you tell me about your dreams?" she asked, amazed at her own sudden boldness.

His eyes gleamed. "Why don't I show you, instead?"

Nerves and anticipation battled inside her. Anticipation won. "Why don't you?" she murmured, lifting her face invitingly to his.

Somehow he managed to kiss her and maneuver her into his bedroom all at the same time.

She'd always known that he was a very resourceful man.

The robe she had knotted so securely opened easily beneath his fingers. His hands slipped inside, drawing her closer until she was pressed against his bare chest. The first jolt of contact made her breath stutter. Her skin felt so cool in contrast to his, so soft and yielding in comparison to his solid strength. But when she felt him tremble, she knew he was as deeply affected by this moment as she was.

Still holding her against him, he kissed her until her knees were weak, until she was incapable of standing upright without clinging to him. And when his strength gave out, as well, they fell together onto the bed. And still he'd done nothing more than hold her, kiss her.

Aching for more, she arched upward. "Touch me, Steve."

"I've waited so long to hear you say that," he murmured, his voice hoarse.

"You can stop waiting. *Touch me.*"

She gasped in relief and pleasure when his hands closed over her breasts. His husky groan expressed his own emotions.

Casey hadn't lost all remnants of her common sense. She wasn't unaware of their unsettled circumstances. She hadn't forgotten the baby sleeping in the other room. She wasn't trying to delude herself that she and Steve were suddenly an ideal couple. But something powerful had been building between them from the day they'd first met, and they'd both known it. All of Casey's resistance hadn't made it go away.

She had wanted him when she'd tried to make herself believe she didn't even like him. Now that she'd spent this weekend with him, and had been forced to acknowledge his kindness, his generosity, his reckless courage and almost quixotic loyalty, she only wanted him more. Maybe it wasn't wise. Maybe it would only lead to disappointment and heartache. She knew full well what her father would say if he were around to see her consorting this way with his competition, and what Edward would think about her recklessness. But it was her choice. Her decision.

If it was a mistake, it was one she was making of her own free will. And the sensation was both heady and liberating.

She ran her hands through Steve's lush, thick brown hair—something she'd always secretly wanted to do. She trailed her fingers down his neck to his broad shoulders, spread her palms against his back and reveled in the heat he generated. Her limbs were fluid and relaxed when he slipped the robe away and pulled her against him. She gave herself over to pleasure, abandoning hesitation. If she was going to go through with this—and she was—she intended to make it a memorable occasion for both of them.

Judging from the murmurs of approval her movements evoked from Steve, she was successful.

She waited impatiently while he stripped off his

jeans, fumbled in the nightstand drawer, and then returned to her. Wrapping her legs around him, she fused her mouth with his as he brought their bodies together with one deep, powerful thrust.

All the rationalizations Casey had used for making love with Steve evaporated—at that moment, she couldn't even form a coherent thought.

Steve tore his mouth from hers, gasping for breath, shuddering with the effort he was making to remain in control. "Casey," he whispered, cupping her face between his hands and raining kisses over her skin. Moving excruciatingly slowly, he murmured endearments to her, telling her how beautiful she was, how badly he had wanted her for so long, telling her that making love with her was even better than he had hoped it would be.

Growing increasingly impatient, she moved eagerly beneath him, running her hands over him, urging him in broken whispers to hurry, to help her, to give them both what they craved so badly.

Steve wouldn't be rushed. "Not yet, darlin'," he breathed, nuzzling her ear. "I've waited too long."

"We have to—" She broke off with a gasp when he made a particularly inspired move, and then she tried again. "We have to hurry. The baby—"

"Isn't going anywhere," he finished for her. "Kiss me, Casey."

She could almost feel her mind empty when his mouth covered hers again, when his tongue swept between her lips to probe, taste, explore. Need was building inside her, clawing its way to the surface. Her movements became more frenetic, more desperate, her hands more greedy as she clutched him, almost begged him to go faster. Deeper. Higher.

She knew the moment she pushed him past the edge of his control. A groan ripped from his chest, vibrating through both of them. And then he gave her exactly what she'd been begging for.

He took her flying. And for once, she wasn't afraid to soar.

STEVE LIFTED HIS HEAD from the pillow with a start. He lay facedown, naked, limbs sprawled. And he was alone.

Blinking his vision into focus, he rolled onto his back, scrubbing one hand over his face. He hadn't meant to go to sleep. He had to blame it on a couple of sleepless nights followed by an interlude of mindblowing sex. Totally knocked him out, he thought wryly.

He glanced at the bedside clock and realized he'd been sleeping for more than an hour. He hoped Casey wasn't annoyed with him for crashing that way. If she was—well, he'd be more than happy to try to make it up to her, he thought with a smile that felt rather smug. Knowing she would be a good deal more than annoyed if she saw him looking a bit too pleased with himself, he smoothed his face and rolled to sit up on the side of the bed.

He needed a shower and food. And then he

needed Casey again. He wondered what the odds were that he would get everything he wanted.

Assuming that Casey was taking care of Annie since he didn't hear crying, he ducked into the bathroom for a quick shower. He left his hair wet, but took the time to shave. Something he should have done before, he thought with a grimace. He hoped he hadn't scraped Casey's soft, delicate skin.

Thinking of Casey—the way her skin had tasted, the way she had felt beneath him and around him—was getting him aroused all over again. It had been too damned long since he'd been with a woman, he thought. He simply hadn't been able to find anyone in recent months who challenged him and intrigued him the way his fiery, beautiful rival had.

Everything was going to be different between them now. He wasn't certain how they would work out their differences—business *or* personal—but he was determined to try. He believed the end results would be worth whatever effort it took to get there. But first, they had to deal with Annie.

Wearing jeans, a knit pullover and sport socks, his still-damp hair swept back from his face with his fingers, he left the bedroom in search of Casey.

He found her in the living room. Dressed in the T-shirt and jeans she'd worn yesterday, she sat in the big rocker with Annie in her arms. She was smiling down at the baby, and singing softly. Annie looked utterly entranced.

Steve knew the feeling. Just looking at Casey now

filled him with so much emotion he could hardly speak. He cleared his tight throat.

The sound brought Casey's gaze to his face. A hint of color stained her cheeks, the only sign that she even remembered what had happened between them just over an hour earlier.

"Annie wanted to get up again," she said. "I changed her diaper, but she doesn't seem to want a bottle yet."

Brusque. Efficient. To the point. If she was making an effort to put them back on their previous footing, he could have told her she was wasting her time. He'd gotten too close to her now. He'd seen the fire and passion she'd been hiding. While he still admired and respected her competence, her intelligence, her unwavering determination to succeed, he'd seen the softer side of her now, as well. And he wasn't going to let her pretend otherwise.

He crossed the room and bent to press a lingering kiss on her lips. "Have you had anything to eat?" he asked when he reluctantly drew away.

Visibly flustered, she shook her head. "No, I..."

"I'll make us some breakfast. What would you like?"

She looked down at the baby. "Whatever you're having will be fine."

He stroked a hand down her hair. It was so silky, so thick. He liked the way she wore it, long and straight to the middle of her back where it ended in a soft wave. "I love your hair," he murmured. "The way it sways when you walk. The way it gleams in the sun. The way it looked spread on my pillow."

Her cheeks went a shade darker. "I—"

He didn't want to give her the chance to downplay what they had shared. "I'll make breakfast," he said, moving toward the kitchen.

That hadn't gone so badly, he mused, pulling eggs and bacon out of the refrigerator. She had tried to act as if nothing out of the ordinary had happened, but he'd seen the truth in her eyes. She was as overwhelmed as he was—she was just trying not to let it show.

She simply needed more time to get used to the idea, he decided.

Annie was still awake by the time he had the meal ready. They strapped her in the plastic infant seat and set it on the table where she could watch them eat. For once, she seemed content not to be held. Sucking her fingers, she kicked her feet and watched them, making an occasional funny noise.

"She hasn't smiled yet," Steve commented, watching the baby's comical expressions.

"I think she's too young. It's, like, a month or six weeks or so before they can consciously smile, isn't it? She's just absorbing all these new images and sensations now."

"Wonder what she thinks when she looks at us?"

Casey made a rueful grimace. "Probably, 'Who are these crazy people and how do I get away from them?'"

Pleased that she'd relaxed enough to make a joke, Steve chuckled. "That's probably exactly what she's thinking."

Having eaten only part of the huge breakfast, Casey pushed her plate away, her smile fading. "She's probably really wondering where her mother is."

As much as he regretted the change in mood, Steve knew it was time to get back to their most pressing problem. Once everything had been settled about Janice and Annie, then they could get back to defining their own relationship.

"I'll call around for Blake again right after breakfast," he said. "I talked to someone last night who had an idea how I could contact him."

"If you can't find him today, we have to call someone else—either another P.I. or the police. Someone. We can't just keep on this way. We both have to work tomorrow, for one thing. And it can't be good for the baby to be so unsettled."

"While I agree that we have to do something soon, I don't think you should be so worried about Annie's welfare. We've been taking good care of her, Casey. She's been fed, bathed, rocked and pampered. I'd say we're doing as well as most couples with their first baby."

"That analogy hardly applies here," she said stiffly.

Maybe not, but Steve didn't find the idea of having children with Casey so far-fetched. Had she really never considered the possibility of a long-term, permanent relationship with him?

Reminding himself that questions like that belonged in the to-be-addressed-later category, he said, "I'm merely pointing out that Annie's safe for the moment. Janice is the one we should be concerned about."

She nodded. "I am. I hated how vulnerable I felt when I discovered I'd been followed last night. I can only imagine what Janice is feeling. And until I know what these people want with her, I'll do whatever I can to keep them from her."

"And so will I." He finished the last of his breakfast and coffee while Casey restlessly cleaned the kitchen. By the time he set his dishes in the dishwasher, no evidence of their meal remained.

"I would like to go home for a little while. I need to call my office and change into clean clothes," she said, running a hand down her T-shirt and jeans. "Will you be okay alone with Annie for a little while?"

"Of course, but I still don't want you going home alone. Let me call B.J.—no," he remembered with a scowl. "B.J.'s running the business today. He has a fairly busy schedule. Maybe I can—"

Casey shook her head. "I don't need an escort," she insisted. "I'm really not afraid, Steve. It's daylight and there are always plenty of people around my apartment on weekends. If I need to, I can scream like a banshee—or so I've been told. I'm not letting some jerk keep me away from my own home any longer."

Steve's smile felt wry. "I don't doubt that you are quite capable of taking care of yourself, Casey, my love. I just can't help worrying about you a little."

Her cheeks flamed—probably in reaction to his using the *L* word, even as casually as he'd tossed it in.

She looked quickly away, her movements flustered. "I need to find my purse and shoes," she muttered, hurrying out of the kitchen. "I—uh—really have to go."

Was she really so anxious to change clothes or was she running from the intimacy they had shared? There was a shadow of panic in her eyes that he suspected had little or nothing to do with lurking strangers.

Later, he reminded himself.

But he *would* confront them eventually. And he fully intended to convince her that her fears were unjustified. He didn't want to hurt her. He didn't want to cause her any trouble.

He only wanted to love her.

9

CARRYING ANNIE IN HER SEAT, Steve followed Casey out of the kitchen into the living room. Though she knew he was watching her, Casey avoided his eyes as she slid her feet into her shoes and snatched up her purse. She was suddenly in a hurry to leave. Her throat was tight, and her chest ached. Oddly enough, she felt like crying, something she very rarely did.

She didn't want to start in front of Steve.

He set the baby carrier on the coffee table and walked with Casey to the door. "I'll see you to your car."

"That really isn't—"

The telephone rang, cutting into her automatic rejection. "Just a second," Steve said, moving toward the phone. "This could be important."

She kept one hand on the doorknob while she waited to find out.

"Oh, hi, Madelyn," he said a moment later. "No, we haven't heard from Janice. Yes, the baby's fine. We're going to..."

Even though she knew he would rather she wait until after he'd finished the call, Casey made a cowardly escape. She gave him a quick wave and slipped out the door, avoiding an awkward farewell or another overprotective gesture on his part.

She hadn't lied to him. She wasn't afraid of going home alone at the moment. But she was *terrified* of facing her feelings for Steve.

She had her hand on the door handle of her car when a man's voice came from behind her. "Excuse me?"

She whirled, her heart leaping into her throat. The man who had appeared out of nowhere was golden-haired and blue-eyed, undeniably handsome, but just slightly dangerous looking. "What do you want?"

His eyes narrowed at her belligerent tone. "I hope you can help me. I'm trying to locate..."

Casey had enough. Three days ago, her life had been hectic, stressful, overly organized, maybe a little unsatisfying, but sane. Safe. She hadn't been partially responsible for the welfare of a helpless infant. She hadn't had to worry about being arrested for concealing a possible crime. She hadn't been afraid to go home in case someone followed her or harassed her by telephone.

And she hadn't been in danger of having her heart broken.

Two days of stress, worry, and sleep deprivation led to an explosion she didn't even try to control. She shoved a finger into the chest of the man who'd had the nerve to impose on her at such an inconvenient time.

"Look, Park or Claybrook or whoever the hell you are—I do *not* know where Janice Gibson is, do you understand? And even if I *did* know, there is nothing you could do or say that would make me tell you. I don't appreciate being followed, harassed or interrogated by rude, obnoxious strangers and I will not tolerate it any further. If you continue to bother me, I'll call the police, and then I'll slap you with a lawsuit that will make your head spin.

"Now," she said, punctuating her words with another sharp jab to his chest, "is there any part of what I've just said that you don't understand?"

Sometime during her tirade, Steve had appeared at her side. Neither of the men tried to interrupt her until she finished. Only when she paused for air did the blond stranger look at Steve with what could only be described as amused admiration.

"If I weren't already happily married, I think I would have just fallen in love," he said, his tone whimsical.

Steve chuckled and wrapped an arm around Casey's shoulders. "I'm crazy about her, myself."

Casey stared first at the stranger, then at Steve. "What...?"

"Casey Jansen, this is Blake," Steve told her gently. "The P.I. I've been trying to reach."

"But I thought you haven't been able to contact him yet."

"I haven't." Steve looked inquiringly at the other man.

Blake shrugged matter-of-factly. "I got word you were looking for me. From what your friend here said, I take it you've got yourself a situation that requires my expertise?"

"You could say that." His left arm still around Casey, Steve extended his right hand to Blake. "Thanks for coming. It's good to see you again."

The warmth with which Blake returned the handshake told Casey he considered Steve a friend. "It's been too long."

"Come in. Let me get you something to drink while we talk. Casey, are you coming in?"

She still wanted to escape for clean clothing and a few hours of solitude to put everything into perspective. But she was compelled to stay and find out what Blake suggested they do about Janice and Annie.

She moved away from Steve's arm and headed toward his house. "I want to hear this," she said over her shoulder.

She would concentrate on Janice's problems for now, she decided, and postpone her own for later. Which meant she would not dwell on the elation she felt hearing Steve say he was "crazy" about her.

Annie was still sitting in the carrier on Steve's coffee table, but she was beginning to squirm and fuss. Casey released the safety straps and lifted the baby into her arms, soothingly patting her back.

Blake looked at the baby in curiosity. "Yours?" he asked, glancing from Casey to Steve.

Though it was a natural assumption, especially considering Steve's earlier comment, Casey felt her cheeks warm anyway.

"No," Steve answered. If he was at all disconcerted by the question, he didn't allow it to show. "This is Annie. She's half the reason we called you."

"Is that right?" Blake stepped closer to Casey and touched a fingertip to Annie's soft cheek. "She's tiny, isn't she?"

"We think she's only a few days old. Less than a week, probably," Casey said.

Blake seemed fascinated by the baby. "My wife and I are expecting our first in a few months," he explained.

"No kidding?" Steve grinned. "I find it hard to picture you as a married man with a kid. Quite a difference from the footloose bachelor I used to know."

"Things change," Blake said with a shrug. "Tara and I have been married for a little more than two years now. I'm still working as an investigator, but I don't travel as much as I did before. I confine my cases mostly to the Atlanta area. That's where we live."

Casey thought it was obvious that Blake was quite content with his life now. She found it interesting that he'd been willing to drop everything and leave his pregnant wife behind when he'd heard that Steve needed him. Just how big a favor had Steve done for this guy?

"Can I get you something to drink, Blake?" Steve

offered as Casey settled into the rocker with the baby.

"Got any coffee?"

"I'll make a fresh pot. It'll only take a few minutes. Make yourself comfortable, I'll be right back."

Blake settled on the couch when Steve left the room. He moved with a grace that Casey couldn't help but admire. His beautifully tailored pale blue shirt and pleated gray slacks emphasized his slender, wiry build. Uncomfortably aware of her own wrinkled, casual clothes, Casey suspected that some women would find Blake irresistible. While she wasn't entirely immune to his attraction, she secretly preferred Steve's more rugged, earthy appeal.

"I'm sorry I startled you outside," Blake said. "I didn't mean to frighten you."

"I should have given you a chance to introduce yourself before I attacked you," she replied. "I mistook you for someone else."

"You mentioned the names Park and Claybrook. Did you mean Frank Claybrook?"

Casey felt her eyes widen. "I think that was the name he used. Do you know him?"

"There's a Frank Claybrook who works as a P.I. out of St. Louis. He's a former prizefighter who doesn't have a lot of scruples about his methods."

"Sounds like the guy I met," Steve said from the doorway. "What about Walter Park? Is that a name you know?"

"There's an investigator named Park who's based

in Springfield, Missouri. Could be the same one, maybe. I don't know every P.I. in the area," Blake admitted with a faint smile.

Steve glanced over his shoulder. "Coffee's ready. I'll be right back."

Blake waited until Steve returned with a tray holding three cups of coffee before asking any more questions. He took an appreciative sip, nodded his approval and then said, "Okay. Shoot."

As succinctly as possible, Steve told him the whole story. Casey spoke up only to add a detail about the phone call she had received at home.

Blake sipped his coffee, looking as if he was hardly paying attention to the tale, but Casey suspected he didn't miss a word. He didn't ask any questions or make any comments until Steve had finished. "Is there anything else?" he asked.

Casey looked at him in surprise. "Isn't that enough?"

His mouth quirked into a crooked smile. "Yes, it's definitely enough. I was just asking if there is anything else I should know."

"Not that I can think of," Steve said. "So, what do you think?"

Blake lifted an eyebrow. "I think you've gotten yourself into a real mess here."

Steve rolled his eyes. "Is that your professional opinion?"

"Mmm. How many people know you've got the baby?"

"As far as we know, only Madelyn, my office manager, and B.J., a company pilot. My neighbor knows there's a baby here—I borrowed a bassinet from her and told her I was baby-sitting for a sick friend."

"She didn't find that odd?"

Steve shrugged. "I don't usually baby-sit, but I have sort of a reputation for doing favors for my friends."

Chuckling, Blake shook his head. "Tell me something I don't know."

"Anyway, that's everyone I can think of. You haven't told anyone, have you, Casey?"

"You know I haven't." Casey answered Steve's question with a frown.

He nodded. "I was just saving Blake the trouble of asking."

Blake glanced at the baby again. "How long are you planning to keep Annie here?"

Again, it was Steve who answered. "We had originally agreed to call the authorities if we hadn't located Janice by this evening. Casey's first instinct was to call the police immediately when we found Annie, but Madelyn, B.J. and I talked her into waiting."

"I only wanted to do what was best for Annie," Casey said a bit defensively. "At the time, I thought the best thing was to turn her over to child protective services."

"You've changed your mind?" Blake asked.

As Annie nestled more snugly into her shoulder,

Casey sighed. "It may still be the sensible thing to do, but I'm not sure I can turn her over now. She's just getting settled here. To give her to strangers, move her from place to place without knowing when, or if, she'll be reunited with her mother—well, I'm just not sure I can accept that now."

"So what we have to do," Blake said almost casually, "is find her mother."

Steve nodded. "That's where we hope you can help us."

"I can't guarantee that I'll find her by tonight. What are you going to do with the kid tomorrow if it takes me a couple of days?"

Steve looked at Casey. She almost groaned. Of the two of them, she knew she was the most able to take a day off from work. She had people to run her operation in her absence, and the paperwork and management decisions that were her responsibility could be postponed or handled off-site. Steve's company was so small that his daily presence was more critical. He didn't have backups available to take over his duties as owner, manager, pilot and instructor. She should, of course, tell him that was his problem— maybe even take advantage of the opportunity to score a few business points against him.

Annie stirred and mewed, making Casey's momentary ruthlessness evaporate. How could she abandon this baby now? And how could she use Steve's own generosity against him? Though she suspected that was exactly what her father would have done, what he would have expected her to do, she simply couldn't do it.

Sorry, Dad. Looks like I'm going to disappoint you again.

"I can stay here and watch her for as long as you need me tomorrow," she said quietly.

The warmth in Steve's smile lit an answering fire deep inside her. "Thank you, Casey," he murmured.

Blake looked from one of them to the other. "So you two are...?"

"Competitors," Casey supplied quickly.

"Close friends," Steve amended. "*Very* close friends."

Casey thought about strangling him. Blake would have to be stupid not to figure out that something was going on between her and Steve. And Blake was not a stupid man.

Fortunately, he seemed to be a discreet one. He asked no more personal questions, but turned the conversation back to Janice. "Is there anything else you can tell me about her?"

Both Steve and Casey explained how little they had known about the young woman who'd worked for them. "I've followed every trail I could think of," Steve added. "I got nowhere."

Blake didn't seem overly concerned. "I'll find her."

"If—when you do," Steve corrected himself, "bring her to us. Whatever it is she's running from, we'll help her."

Blake glanced at Casey. "You feel the same way?"

"Of course," she answered, almost annoyed that he had asked. Was Blake, like so many others, misinterpreting her natural reserve for coldness?

He gave her a nod that seemed to express approval. "Looks like Janice had good reason to believe she was putting her baby in safe hands."

Casey didn't tell him that Janice had technically left the child with Steve, not her. She saw no need to mention it at the moment—especially since she'd become as entangled in this situation as Steve. And almost as willingly.

Blake set his empty mug on the coffee table and stood. "I'll be in touch when I have something for you."

"Just like that?" Casey asked.

He smiled at her. "Remind me sometime to tell you about the favor Steve once did for me."

He leaned over to bring his face into Annie's line of view. "See you later, beautiful. And I'll have your mom with me when I return, okay?"

Casey would have almost sworn that Annie cooed in gratitude. This guy really was dangerous—in many ways, she decided.

A moment later, he was gone.

Looking at Steve, Casey asked, "Do you think he'll find her?"

"What do *you* think?"

She gave it a moment's consideration. "I think he probably will."

"So do I. By the way, it was very generous of you to offer to watch Annie tomorrow. I know how difficult the offer must have been for you."

"I made it for Annie, not for you," she said a bit gruffly.

He moved to stand beside her chair, stroking her hair. He seemed to enjoy doing that, she thought. She wondered if he knew that he made her tremble every time he did it.

"You talk so tough," he murmured, a smile in his voice. "But this time I don't believe you. You know full well that Annie will be fine—that I'd make arrangements to stay with her myself if you couldn't. But you also know how difficult it is for me to be away from my office for a day. Your offer was for me, not Annie. And I appreciate it."

Casey tried to frown at him. "Don't be ridiculous. Why would I help you stay in business when I fully intend to put you under?"

He leaned over to brush a kiss against her lips. "When you come up with the answer to that, be sure and let me know."

That whisper of a kiss had only left her hungry for more. She averted her eyes before he could read the truth there. "Annie's going to want her bottle soon."

"I'll get one ready." He seemed to understand that she needed some time and space to analyze her own emotions.

She was both grateful and inexplicably disappointed when he moved away from her.

WHEN CASEY finally returned to her apartment an hour later, she had the strangest sensation that she'd been gone much longer than one night. So much had happened since she'd left here yesterday, she thought, a bit dazed. Would anything ever be quite the same again?

There'd been no evidence of anyone following her this time, and she'd seen no one lurking outside her door. Ignoring the blinking message light on her answering machine for the moment, she headed straight for her bedroom, where she changed into clean clothes and touched up what little makeup she'd been able to apply from her purse that morning. She put her hair up in a neat twist, then made a cursory examination of her reflection in the mirror.

She looked as though she was headed for the office in her black slacks and black-and-red print blouse. For some reason, she felt more confident and prepared for the rest of the day now that she was more professionally dressed.

Only then did she feel ready to face her messages. She pushed the play button. The first two messages were from JCS employees; she made a note to call them back. The third message was from an old friend who wanted to schedule a catch-up dinner. Scribbling down the number, she began to relax when it seemed that all the calls had been innocuous.

And then a man's voice came through the speaker. "Ms. Jansen, this is Frank Claybrook. I'm an investigator looking for a former employee of yours, Janice

Gibson. I've tried to reach you at your office, but your employees say you've been unavailable this weekend. I'd appreciate it if you'd call me as soon as you get this. You can leave a message at the Discount Inn on Ninth Street." He concluded by reciting the motel telephone number and then adding a brusque, "Thank you."

"Forget it, Claybrook," Casey muttered, not bothering to write down the number. "I have no intention of calling you."

She spent the next forty-five minutes concentrating on business, making arrangements with her staff in case she couldn't get in the following day. "If you need to reach me, call my cell phone number," she instructed her office manager, making a mental note to keep the phone nearby. She didn't want to give out Steve's number—just in case there was any way someone might figure out where she'd been spending so much time lately.

Seemingly unperturbed at being contacted on a Sunday afternoon, the efficient Pamela replied, "Yes, Ms. Jansen. And if Jack Alexander calls?"

It suddenly occurred to Casey that no one on her staff called her by her first name. Not her office workers, her pilots, or her maintenance people. She'd known some of them since her childhood, yet they called her Ms. Jansen—just as they'd called her father Mr. Jansen. She had never thought to suggest otherwise.

Would any of them feel free to come to her if they

were in trouble? Somehow she doubted it—just as she couldn't imagine turning to any of them with her personal problems.

How much had she sacrificed to prove to her father that she could be as capable as he was?

"Ms. Jansen?" Pamela repeated. "What shall I tell Mr. Alexander if he calls?"

"Give him my cell number," Casey answered. "Whatever I'm doing, I'll make time to talk to him." Alexander was a successful distributor whose business Casey had been after for some time. She'd been trying to convince him to use her charter service rather than the big-name carriers he'd patronized in the past.

"Is there anything else?"

"No, that will be all," Casey replied. After a moment's hesitation, she added, "Pamela—thank you. I'm sorry I had to disturb you on your day off."

"That's quite all right, Ms. Jansen." Pamela sounded just a bit surprised.

It probably wouldn't hurt her to study Steve's management skills a bit, at least in the area of employee relations, Casey mused as she hung up the phone. Of course, her father would have scoffed at the very idea.

She knew she should head back to Steve's place soon. Though he seemed to be taking good care of the baby, he could probably use some assistance. She knew he probably needed a load of laundry done, especially towels and the baby's sleepers. But she wasn't quite ready to go back.

The truth was, she thought, sinking to the couch, she was terrified of her feelings for Steve. And she wasn't entirely sure why.

Of course there were the fears that accompanied any new relationship. Were his feelings genuine? Did he want a future with her or only a fling? Had he seen her as a challenge whose appeal to him would wane now that he'd succeeded in charming her into his bed?

But there were other fears in this case. No matter how casually Steve seemed to run his business, Casey knew exactly how hard he had worked, how many hours he had invested. Beneath his lazy smiles was a determination that had made him a formidable competitor in a relatively short time. She knew how badly he wanted Lockhart Air to succeed—but how far was he willing to go to make sure it did so? There was no denying his unswerving loyalty to his own employees, but did he feel any responsibility to his competitor, even a competitor he desired on a physical level?

Her father had not taught her to trust blindly.

She'd spent so many years in her father's shadow, trying to prove herself to him. And later trying to prove to everyone else that she was equal to him. She had only recently begun to feel that she had finally asserted her independence, that she had finally begun to build a life of her own.

Steve was very different from Louis Jansen in many ways, but there were a few traits the two men shared. Like Louis, Steve was larger-than-life, a man others instinctively followed, a man who couldn't be relegated to the background. Like Louis, he was accustomed to making his own rules, following his own agenda, having his own way.

How would he feel about Casey if she really *did* succeed in putting him out of business?

It looked to her as if this whole situation was headed for disaster. Was she ready to risk that just when she'd begun to feel she had her future under control?

10

By THE TIME Casey returned to Steve's house late that afternoon, she was confident that she knew exactly what to say to him. She had needed some time on her own, she decided. It had given her a chance to put everything into perspective. To remind herself of her priorities. To convince herself that nothing had really changed just because she and Steve had given in to a fleeting impulse.

That itch had been scratched, she assured herself firmly, if a bit indelicately. It wouldn't happen again. By now, Steve had probably come to the same conclusion.

They were both too busy and much too different to attempt a serious relationship. They were rivals, enemies. She had vowed to crush him, and he had insisted he wouldn't allow her to do so. It was ridiculous to consider there could be anything more between them.

She was quite sure Steve would agree if she explained it just that way.

Carrying a bag of groceries for dinner, she approached his front door. An adhesive-backed note had been stuck beneath the doorbell. She smiled when she read the words scribbled on it: *Baby sleeping. Do not ring bell.*

Apparently, Annie hadn't gone down easily for her nap.

Casey tapped lightly on the door. Steve opened it almost immediately. "I just got her to sleep," he said with a slightly worn smile. "Her Highness has not been in the best of moods."

"Do you think something is wrong?" Casey asked in concern, immediately conjuring up a whole list of dangerous childhood illnesses.

Steve reached out to take the grocery bag from her. "I think she was missing you," he said. "Something I completely understand."

That comment, while rather sweet, gave her the perfect opening. "Steve—"

"I'll take these things into the kitchen. Did you have lunch?"

"Yes, a couple of hours ago. Did you?"

"Mmm. I grabbed a sandwich while Annie was resting between tantrums."

Casey bit her lip, feeling a bit guilty because she'd left him alone with the baby for so long. And then she reminded herself that she had baby-sat most of the day yesterday and had volunteered to do so again tomorrow.

"Steve," she said again, following him into the kitchen. "There's something I—"

He was already unloading the bag. "Looks like the ingredients for lasagna."

"Yes. I thought you might be getting tired of take-out."

"Sounds great. I love lasagna." He stashed the perishable items in the refrigerator, leaving everything else on the counter. And then he turned to smile at her. "I don't know what I would have done without you this weekend, Casey."

His deep, intimate tone made her knees go weak. She stiffened them resolutely. "Yes, well, someone had to give you a hand with the baby and it was obvious that there was no one else available."

"There's definitely no one else I'd rather have had with me," he murmured, reaching out to stroke her cheek with his knuckles.

She swallowed, aware that this talk wasn't going exactly as she had planned. "Steve, we need to—"

"Do you know how long it has been since I kissed you?" His tone was almost whimsical now, though the expression in his eyes was anything but. "Hours. But it seems like days."

"That's..." She cleared her throat. "That's what I wanted to talk to you about."

He bent his head to brush his lips across the tip of her nose. "Why waste time talking when there are so many better things we can do?"

His lips captured hers before she could launch into her carefully prepared speech.

It seemed like a very long time before the kiss ended. Steve lifted his head a few inches—as far as he could with Casey's arms locked tightly around his neck. She wondered dazedly when she had placed them there.

Sliding his hands slowly down her back, he rested his forehead against hers with a slight sigh. "Do you have any idea what you do to me?"

What *she* did to *him*? All he had to do was smile at her and her mind emptied of rational thought. A mere touch of his hand could make her tremble. And when he kissed her, when he held her like this, he made her want everything she had convinced herself she could never have.

"There was something I wanted to tell you," she said, tilting her head to a better angle when he began to nuzzle her ear.

"What is it?" He seemed more interested in what he was doing than in what she was saying.

She sagged against him when the tip of his tongue circled her ear. "I...um...needed to tell you what I..." Her voice broke off in a moan when his left hand closed over her right breast, his thumb slowly circling through her clothing.

He'd raised his right hand to the back of her head. She felt a couple of tugs and then her hair tumbled around her shoulders and onto her back. "What were you saying?" he encouraged, speaking against her lips.

She was going to tell him not to do this any more, she reminded herself. That she didn't want this. That they were all wrong for each other. Maybe, she thought as his mouth moved enticingly over hers, maybe she could tell him later. She tightened her arms around his neck and parted her lips for him, deciding there was no real hurry, after all.

Some time later, he lifted his mouth again, giving them both a chance to breathe, if somewhat raggedly. The smile that crossed his sexy mouth was pure temptation. "Annie should sleep awhile yet."

She knew what he was hinting at, of course. All the sensible arguments she'd formulated that afternoon echoed in her mind. They were all still very logical, all completely valid. She still believed every one of them.

But would it really be so awful if she said them later? If she gave herself one last opportunity to pretend that things could be different between them?

"How much longer?" she murmured, resting a hand against Steve's warm, strong jaw.

He caught her hand and placed a gentle kiss in her palm. "Long enough," he muttered. "I want you, Casey."

"I want you, too," she said with a soft sigh of surrender. That was one fact she couldn't deny, no matter how foolish it might be.

A moment later, she found herself in his arms, being carried toward the bedroom. Never in her life had a man carried her to bed. Never in her life had she believed she would have liked it. Had she known what a thrill it would be, she might have incorporated it into a few more fantasies.

"The baby?" she remembered to ask.

"I put the bassinet in the spare bedroom this time," he murmured, laying Casey on the bed and following her down. "The door is open. We'll be able to hear her if she wants us."

Relieved of that concern, Casey allowed herself to concentrate on Steve. He seemed intent on studying every inch of her this time, and she was in an accommodating mood. The prim, neat clothing she'd donned as symbolic armor fell away beneath Steve's skillful fingers, leaving her completely revealed to him.

He buried his face in her throat, nuzzling against the pulse that raced in the hollow there. And then he slid lower, his mouth skimming her chest, then closing over the straining tip of her right breast. Casey buried her fingers in his lush hair and arched beneath him. He murmured something that might have been an endearment, might have been encouragement—might have been something else. She didn't try to decipher it.

He nibbled her tummy, causing her to squirm with both pleasure and acute sensitivity. He circled her navel with the tip of his tongue, tickling her and making her laugh, and then he moved even lower, making her gasp with sensations so intense they took her breath away.

By the time he donned protection from his nightstand and then returned to her, Casey was almost frantic with need. She drew him down to her impatiently, wrapping herself around him, welcoming him eagerly when he thrust into her.

Once again, he took her flying. And she felt incredibly bold and safe, because Steve was with her all the way.

OKAY, CASEY MUSED when her mind cleared enough to let her form coherent thought again. So today hadn't gone exactly as she had planned. It wasn't too late to start getting it back on track.

She lifted her cheek from Steve's bare shoulder. He stirred beneath her, opening heavy-lidded eyes. "Where are you going?"

"To check on the baby."

"I'm sure she's fine. She'll let us know when she wants something."

"I'd like to check on her, anyway." Even though it was the truth, it also made a good excuse for her to put some distance between herself and Steve. Lying here naked in his arms was a feeling that was almost painful in its intensity. She had a sneaking suspicion that it might become addictive.

"One minute more," Steve murmured, drawing her mouth to his for another lingering kiss. Only then did he release her with visible reluctance.

The neat, prim-looking clothes she'd donned so purposefully earlier were now scattered all over the floor. She gathered them self-consciously and escaped to the bathroom, away from Steve's too-perceptive gaze.

She dressed quickly, fastening every button, tucking her blouse in tightly. There was nothing she could do about her hair except shake it straight down her back. The pins that had held it in the neat twist she'd worn earlier were probably scattered all over Steve's house.

Already she was berating herself for her lapse of willpower. If she couldn't remain firm in her resistance for one day, how was she going to do so in the upcoming weeks?

Needing a distraction, she tiptoed into the guest room to the bassinet. Annie wasn't fully awake, but she was beginning to stir, bumping her head against the mattress beneath her and making funny little noises.

Infants certainly demanded a great deal of time and attention. It was probably just as well that she wasn't likely to have one of her own anytime soon, she thought.

"You're running again," Steve said from the doorway.

She looked at him over the bassinet. He'd donned his jeans and pullover and had run a hand through his hair, but he still looked as though he'd just climbed out of bed. "What are you talking about?" she asked, dragging her gaze away from him.

"Every time I think you and I are getting close, you run—emotionally, if not physically. What are you so afraid of, Casey?"

Of you, she wanted to tell him. *Of losing myself in*

you just when I'm learning how to be the confident, self-sufficient woman I always wanted to be.

"I'm not afraid of anything," she answered.

"Casey—"

Annie whimpered and opened her eyes.

Casey reached for the baby almost gratefully. "She probably needs a clean diaper. I'll change her."

"Hiding behind a baby?"

She sent a quick frown in Steve's direction. "This really isn't the time for a discussion about us, Steve. We have more pressing things to concentrate on now."

"Perhaps," he murmured, "but we will have to talk about this soon. It won't simply go away if you ignore it."

Probably not, Casey thought, laying Annie on the bed and reaching for baby wipes and a clean diaper. But it seemed worth a try—at least for now.

When Annie was clean and dry again, Casey handed her to Steve. "I'll start dinner," she said, not quite meeting his eyes.

"Casey..."

She could tell he wasn't quite ready to let it go. "Steve, please. I need some time."

He sighed. "You're making me crazy, you know."

She didn't smile. "I know."

It went both ways, of course. Steve Lockhart was making her crazy, too. How else could she explain the way she kept ending up in bed with him, despite her utter certainty that it was a disastrous mistake?

The problem was, it always seemed like a good idea at the time.

STEVE COULD HEAR CASEY moving around in the kitchen, and from the aromas emanating from there, he assumed dinner was almost ready. He'd taken the hint that she wanted to be left alone while she cooked, so he sat in the rocking chair in the living room with Annie, who'd just taken a bottle and was now lying in his arms making faces and sucking her fingers.

"When you grow up," he murmured to the baby, "and you become a beautiful, intelligent, incredibly desirable woman—as I'm sure you will—are you going to turn some man inside out and leave his head spinning with your unpredictable behavior?"

Annie gurgled, sounding rather pleased by the prospect.

"Women," Steve said with a sigh, shaking his head.

Annie grunted softly, making him chuckle. He liked sitting here like this, holding her, watching the funny faces she made. It gave him an odd feeling to think that his footloose old friend Blake would be a father in a few months. Steve hadn't given a lot of thought to fatherhood, himself, but he'd been thinking about it quite a bit this weekend. He thought he'd be pretty good at it. And he wanted it more than he'd ever realized before.

He wanted to experience it with Casey, he

thought, his heart swelling with the magnitude of the emotions growing inside him.

He wished he could understand what she was thinking, what she was feeling at this moment. He had always suspected that she hid a passionate and volatile nature behind the cool, professional exterior she revealed to most people. He had been utterly delighted to discover that he'd been right—but now how was he supposed to convince her that it was safe to let him get to know that side of her?

It had to be fear that made her pull back every time he thought they were making headway. Fear that he would hurt her. Fear of her own feelings. Fear of endangering the business her father had entrusted to her. Maybe all of the above.

While he could understand that to a point, he wasn't going to give in to it. Casey had to realize that he would never hurt her. He was crazy in love with her, and had been for months. If she didn't know that by now, it was time for him to make it very clear to her. And he didn't know if he could wait until the situation with Annie and Janice was fully resolved before he made his intentions clear.

He wasn't a patient man, and he wasn't one who could simply set his feelings aside until a convenient time arose to deal with them.

She appeared in the kitchen doorway. "Dinner's almost ready," she said without quite meeting his eyes. He doubted that the high color on her cheeks was entirely due to the heat of the kitchen.

"It smells great."

She glanced at the baby. "Do you think she'll sit in her carrier while we eat again?"

"We can try. She seems to be in a pretty good mood for the moment."

The faintest smile touched Casey's lips as she continued to look at Annie. "So it seems."

Casey had definitely developed a soft spot for this baby, Steve thought. He wondered how she felt about having a few kids of her own.

Knowing that this would be the wrong time to ask that question, he kept it to himself. At least for now.

He was just rising from the rocking chair when the telephone rang. Sinking back into the seat, he cradled Annie in his left arm and reached for the receiver with his right hand. Casey moved a step closer, obviously wanting to discover if the call held any news of Janice.

"Hello?"

"Hi, Steve, it's Blake."

Steve nodded to Casey, indicating that she should stay close. "What have you got for us, Blake?"

"I haven't found Janice yet. But I've learned a great deal about her."

"Such as?"

"Janice Gibson is her real name. She grew up in St. Louis, the youngest offspring of a well-off but apparently very restrictive couple. She had some behavior problems in her teens—they sounded to me like classic youthful rebellion, nothing major. She enrolled in college when she was eighteen, but dropped out after two years, a decision her parents vehemently opposed. And then a couple of years ago, she hooked up with a guy named Rick Walls."

Steve could tell from Blake's tone that he didn't consider that a positive development in Janice's life. "Is that Annie's father?"

"Unfortunately, yes. The guy's bad news, Steve. Got a problem with the bottle. And with his temper. Combine the two, and he's dangerous."

Steve scowled. "Dangerous to Janice?"

"To anyone who gets in his way. I contacted someone who knew Janice a year ago, and she told me that Janice tried to leave the guy several times. He always brought her back, probably with threats. She disappeared just over six months ago, and he's been looking for her ever since."

"She got out when she realized she was pregnant," Steve speculated.

"Probably."

"Why didn't she go to her family? The police?"

"Her parents basically disowned her when she got involved with Walls in the first place. They despised him and wanted nothing to do with her if she wouldn't take their advice. She probably doubted that they would help her if she showed up carrying Walls's baby. As for the police, well, she filed several complaints against him the year before she left him. Nothing was ever done, and eventually she dropped each complaint. God knows what he threatened.

Trust me, Steve, I've seen enough domestic violence situations to know that the woman often feels as if she has absolutely no one to turn to."

"So what do you think made her leave Annie with me and take off the way she did?"

"I think Walter Park must have contacted her. He's working for Walls, by the way. It was either he or Walls who most likely followed Casey yesterday, since Walls is in town. If Janice thought Walls had located her and the baby, she probably panicked, left the baby with you for safekeeping and took off."

"Park is working for Walls? Then who hired Claybrook, the guy who approached me?"

"Janice's family. The woman I talked to, the one who told me about Janice's history with Walls, said she contacted them when Janice disappeared. She knew about the baby, though she didn't think Walls did at the time. She thought Janice's family should have the option to try to help her, if they would."

"And they're willing to do so?"

"They hired Claybrook," Blake said in reply.

"You don't suppose she's contacted them this weekend?"

"No. I talked to her mother. She doesn't know where Janice is."

"Did you tell her about the baby?"

"Of course not. If anyone knows you have Annie, they didn't hear it from me."

"Do you have any idea where Janice could be now?"

"I have a few leads. I'll find her."

"You've made a lot of progress in an amazingly short time. I'm impressed."

Blake laughed softly. "It's my job, Steve. I know what I'm doing."

"I never doubted it."

"I'll get back to you as soon as I know more. In the meantime, how's the kid?"

"The kid's great," Steve said with a glance at the tiny baby in his arms.

"And Casey?"

"Casey's great, too." Steve winked at her as he said it, and was pleased to see her blush. He just loved it when she did that.

"Yeah, well, kiss 'em both for me."

"I'll be sure to do that."

"I doubt that you'll find it a chore," Blake said dryly.

Steve laughed. "You've got that right."

Casey looked very impatient by the time Steve hung up the phone. "Well? Has Blake found Janice?"

"He hasn't found Janice," Steve answered. "But he's answered one big question. We now know why Janice is running."

CASEY DIDN'T LINGER long after dinner. "If I'm going to be here with the baby tomorrow, there are a few things I need to do at home tonight."

"I was kind of hoping you'd spend the night,"

Steve said invitingly. "We've hardly had a chance to even talk about us tonight."

They'd spent the entire evening talking about other things—Blake's phone call and the disturbing information it had contained about Janice's past and Annie's parentage. Although there had been good reason to discuss those issues, Casey had also been very careful to avoid a more personal tête-à-tête with Steve tonight. She needed to strengthen her resolve against him.

She shook her head and tucked her purse beneath her arm. "You're perfectly capable of taking care of her yourself tonight. I didn't help you at all with her last night."

"I want you to stay because of me, not because of Annie."

She cleared her throat. "I'd really better go. I'll be back in the morning to relieve you."

"Running again," he murmured. "When are you going to trust me, Casey, darlin'?"

Because there was no easy answer to that, considering she didn't even trust herself where he was concerned, she didn't bother to make an attempt. "Good night, Steve. Call if you need me."

"I need you."

"Or," she said, determinedly ignoring him, "if you hear anything more about Janice."

He nodded in resignation. "I'm not going to change your mind about staying, am I?"

"No." She reached for the doorknob.

"Then I won't try anymore—tonight. But, Casey, I *will* try again."

She was aware of that. She only hoped she would be as resolute next time he asked.

On that thought, she fled.

Once again, she arrived home without incident. No cars followed her, and there were no weird messages on her answering machine. Her apartment was tidy, quiet, peaceful. A little lonely, perhaps, but safe.

She was perfectly content, she assured herself firmly.

Close to exhaustion, she went to bed, but she slept only fitfully. She kept waking up, certain she heard a baby crying, thinking she needed to tend to Annie.

Only Annie wasn't there.

Once, she woke up reaching out to the other side of the bed, as if hoping to find someone there. Since she knew exactly who she'd been dreaming about, she was extremely annoyed with herself. This was hardly the way to get Steve out of her system.

Yet how was she supposed to control her dreams?

She rolled over, punched the pillow, and pulled the covers to her chin. She could handle this, she told herself grimly. Closing her eyes, she tried to will herself back to sleep. She could put Steve out of her life *and* her dreams, she told herself.

She only hoped she could put him out of her heart, as well.

11

"YOU'RE SURE you'll be all right with Annie today?"
Steve seemed reluctant to leave.

Casey was practically pushing him out the door.
During the fifteen minutes that had passed since
she'd arrived, she'd managed to avoid any kisses or
other intimacies that Steve had tried to initiate, and
was rather pleased with herself. The only real diffi-
culty she was having was convincing him to leave.

"Annie and I will be fine. I am perfectly capable of
taking care of her. Now go, before I change my mind
about giving you a hand today. It would serve you
right if I left you to deal with Annie *and* your penny-
ante charter service."

"Penny ante?" A gleam of humor replaced the
concern in his eyes. "Excuse me?"

"You heard me, Lockhart. Now go. Shoo. Scat.
And keep your grubby paws away from my clients."

"That tears it." He reached out and jerked her into
his arms. He kissed her firmly, thoroughly, then
lifted his head to grin down at her, his eyes gleaming. "I'm certifiably crazy about you, Casey Jansen."

The morning had been going so well until that
point. She'd had everything so neatly under control.

But with only a kiss and a few well-spoken words, Steve had just shattered her complacency. She could think of absolutely nothing to say except, "Go away."

"I will," he said with a chuckle. "But, darlin'—I'll be back."

She closed the door behind him, locked it, then sagged against it, resting her forehead on the wood. Maybe she should start rethinking this situation with Steve, she thought with a sigh of surrender. Maybe there was the slimmest chance that they could be together for a while longer, after all.

I'm certifiably crazy about you, Casey Jansen. The words echoed in her mind, making her shiver all over again.

"Jansen," she muttered into the unresponsive door. "You're an idiot."

From the bassinet, Annie began to cry. Relieved to have something to occupy her time, Casey straightened and hurried into the other room to get the baby.

Annie did not stop crying for the next two hours. She cried when she was held. She screamed when Casey laid her down. She didn't want a bottle. Her diaper was dry. Rocking and singing didn't soothe her.

Casey was becoming frantic. Was it colic or something more serious? The baby didn't seem feverish, and as far as Casey could tell, she wasn't in pain. Was it normal for a baby to cry this much and for so long?

She took some encouragement when Annie finally subsided into unhappy whimpers, but ten minutes later it started again. Casey was almost ready to sit down on the floor and cry along. Her nerves were on edge and her ears buzzed from the high-pitched squalls. She wished she knew someone to call for advice, but the few friends she'd had time to make in the past year or so were single, childless career women like herself.

As much as she hated to admit defeat, she was on the verge of calling Steve and asking for help when the telephone rang. At first, she thought maybe he'd sensed her distress and was calling to check on her. And then she realized it was her cell phone ringing, not Steve's house phone.

Jiggling Annie wearily in her left arm, she lifted the phone to her ear. "Hello?"

"Ms. Jansen, it's Pamela. I called to tell you...um, is that a baby crying?"

"Yes. Pamela, you have children?"

Though the statement was obvious, Pamela agreed politely. "Yes. Three of them."

"Does this sound normal to you?" Casey held the phone toward Annie for a moment, then returned it to her ear. "She's been doing that for the past two hours."

"How old is she?"

"About a week."

"Then, yes, it's probably normal. They get tummy aches sometimes. Gas bubbles. And sometimes they just seem to have crying spells for no apparent reason. My mother-in-law always said it helps them expand their lung power."

"I don't think this kid's lacking in the lung power area." Casey muttered.

"I'm sorry, Ms. Jansen, I can't hear you very well."

Casey raised her voice to be heard over the noise Annie was making. "Do you have any suggestions?"

"You're asking *me* for advice?" For the first time, Pamela sounded a bit flustered. "Um—my babies always seemed to settle down when I laid them on their tummies across my knees and rubbed their backs. I don't know why, but it almost always worked."

"It's worth a shot." Juggling the little phone, Casey shifted Annie into the position Pamela had recommended.

"If she doesn't stop crying soon, you should probably call a doctor. She could be ill. But it's more likely just a tummy ache, especially if she's on formula."

"She is. Thanks, Pamela." Annie had not stopped crying yet, but the volume was decreasing. She seemed to be calming a bit in response to Casey's soothing backrub.

"You're welcome." Discreet as always, Pamela didn't ask any questions about why Casey was missing a day of work to take care of a baby. "About the reason I called..."

"Oh, yes. What is it? Have you heard from Mr. Alexander?"

"Well...yes. In a way."

With most of her attention on Annie, who seemed to be whimpering herself to sleep, Casey asked, "What does that mean?"

"Mr. Alexander has gone to contract with Lockhart Air."

Casey went very still. Only her fear of startling Annie kept Casey from shouting *"What?"* Instead, she took several deep, forceful breaths and made herself speak in a low, controlled voice. "Are you certain about that?"

"I'm afraid so. He had his secretary call to inform us of his decision."

Casey felt as if she had just taken a physical blow. She had begun to trust Steve, she realized. And he'd used that trust against her. What a fool she had been. "Did he give a reason?" she asked, speaking with great effort.

"He merely said that after interviewing and researching both companies, he chose to give his business to Lockhart."

"I was the one who convinced him to consider air charter in the first place," Casey said from between clenched teeth. "Until I started talking to him, he was committed to road freight."

"I'm sorry, Ms. Jansen." Pamela didn't seem to know what else to say.

"If I hadn't been away from the office all weekend— If I'd been able to talk to him before he made his final decision—" Losing Alexander was a devastating blow. His account would have put JCS back on the solid financial footing Casey had been working so hard to achieve.

"I'm not sure you could have changed his mind," Pamela replied gently. "His secretary said he was quite certain this is what he wanted to do."

"Lockhart got to him," Casey muttered, wondering what, exactly, Steve had promised this time. How he must be laughing now that he'd charmed both her and Jack Alexander, all in the same weekend.

"I assume so."

"But how did he *know?*" Casey was talking more to herself now than to her assistant. "I never mentioned Alexander to him. Unless—"

She thought of the paperwork she'd worked on at Steve's house on Saturday. She'd had a briefcase full of notes and files, including several bid options she'd worked up for Jack Alexander. Was it possible that Steve had…?

"I'll strangle him if I find out he did anything like that," she muttered furiously.

"I beg your pardon?"

"Never mind. Is there anything else, Pamela?"

"No. I thought you would want to know about Mr. Alexander immediately."

"You were right. Thank you. And by the way…"

"Yes, Ms. Jansen?"

"Never mind," she muttered again. She had almost suggested that Pamela should start calling her

Casey. But then she'd decided that she had no intention of mimicking Steve's business management practices. Any of them. What she was doing now had worked for her father and her grandfather, she told herself as she set the phone aside. It would work for her, as well.

At least until Steve Lockhart succeeded in putting her out of business altogether.

STEVE HAD JUST WALKED into his office early that afternoon after flying a team of accountants to Springfield when Madelyn looked up from the telephone receiver in her hand. "Ms. Jansen is on line two," she said, pushing the hold button. "She wants to talk to you *immediately.*"

The way she'd stressed the last word made Steve's stomach tighten. "Is something wrong?" he asked quickly. "Is it the baby?"

Madelyn shook her head. "She said the baby's fine. She wants to talk to you about a business matter. And Steve—she sounded mad."

"She always sounds mad when she talks about business," Steve said, relieved that there was no real emergency. He suspected that Casey's attitude toward running her business was a result of her lack of true enthusiasm for the job. Steve found real joy in his work. He had a true passion for flying. "Joy" and "passion" were suspiciously absent from Casey's view of the career her father had guilt-talked her into.

He would hate to think that Casey felt trapped in a position she had never truly wanted. How could anyone be truly happy in that situation? And he wanted very badly for Casey to be happy.

He moved into his office and closed the door before picking up the phone and punching the button for line two. "Casey?"

"Steve." Her voice was so cold that he knew immediately how Madelyn had known she was annoyed.

He kept his tone deliberately cheerful. "How's everything going, darlin'? Baby Annie's doing okay?"

"She screamed nonstop for more than two hours this morning. She's sleeping now."

He winced. Casey was obviously not having a good day. "She seems okay now? You don't think she's getting sick or anything?"

"She's fine. I think she had a touch of colic. When will you be back?"

The abrupt change of subject made him blink before answering. "The usual time, I guess. Five-ish. Unless you need me sooner?"

"As soon as you can get here. I have things to do, too, you know. And tomorrow you're going to have to make other arrangements. I really must get back to my office."

There was something going on here besides Annie's temper tantrum. Steve wondered how he could find out what it was. "Uh...did you get a call from your office? Is your absence causing a problem there?"

"Apparently, my absence has cost me a valuable potential customer. It seems he decided to go with the competition instead."

Steve grimaced and cleared his throat. Since he *was* the competition, he now knew why Casey was upset. "Um—which potential customer would that be?" he asked carefully.

"Jack Alexander."

"Alexander?" Steve repeated the name in surprise. "I didn't even realize—"

"How could you do that to me, Steve?" Her voice had risen now and had changed from frosty to fiery. "I've spent all weekend helping you with the baby—going out of my way so your business wouldn't suffer just because you'd done a generous and unselfish favor for someone—and *this* is how you pay me back? It must have been very convenient for you to have me busy here with Annie while you did everything you could to drive me out of business."

"Casey—"

"I *trusted* you. I thought you would agree that the rivalry was off until this situation was settled. I never thought you would use Annie—use *me*—to get ahead."

"Casey, now come on. You know better than that."

"What I know," she snapped, "is that I spent months convincing Alexander that air charter was

the way to go with his business. I wined him and
dined him and spent hours working up proposals
and bid sheets for him. And the first time I was away
from the office—doing a favor for *you*, of course—
you moved right in and stole him from me. God
knows what you promised him—or how you got
your hands on my figures so you could underbid
me."

"Now, just a minute—"

"Just don't come to me for any more favors, Lockhart. You can bet I won't ask any of you!" She dis-
connected with a crash that made his ears ring.

"Damn it, Casey," he protested to the dial tone.
"That was really unfair."

He had no intention of letting it go at that, of
course. He pushed away from the desk and strode
across the office, jerking open the door. "Madelyn,
I'm out for the rest of the day. Handle things for me,
will you?"

She blinked a couple of times, the only indication
of her dismay at being left to cancel appointments
and reschedule lessons. "Okay, Steve."

"Thanks, Madelyn. I owe you."

"Yes. You do." She smiled faintly as she picked up
the telephone. "Good luck, Steve," she called after
him.

"Thanks. I'm going to need it," he muttered, head-
ing for his car.

Casey would soon find out that he had no intention of letting her go easily now that they had finally gotten together.

TWENTY MINUTES after slamming the phone into its cradle, Casey was still furious. She tried to rein in her anger so she wouldn't upset Annie, but it wasn't easy.

"I want you to know," she told the baby lying blessedly quietly in her arms, "that this has nothing to do with you. You are a precious, adorable child, and you don't deserve anything that has happened to you in the past few days. If there were any way I could take you home and watch you there, I would, but I don't have anyone to take care of you while I work. And I really must get back to work."

Annie blinked at her.

"I'm not trying to get away from you," Casey assured her. "Even after the tantrum you threw this morning, I still don't really mind taking care of you. It's been very interesting, actually. I've never had a chance to spend time with a baby before, and I've enjoyed it, for the most part. It may well be the last time I have an opportunity like this," she added somberly.

And then she drew a deep breath. "But even if I can't be with you any more, I don't want you to worry. Steve will do whatever is necessary to take care of you. He might be a complete jerk when it comes to business, but he would never do anything to put you at risk. When it comes to your safety and comfort, Steve can be trusted completely."

She swallowed painfully, her eyes burning as she thought of how foolish *she* had been to trust him.

She wouldn't cry, she assured herself. That wasn't her style. When Steve arrived, she would hand him the baby, bid him a cool goodbye, and leave without another word. She wouldn't give him the satisfaction of losing her temper again, or falling apart in front of him.

She would wait until she got home to do that.

Heavy footsteps on the front porch brought her head up. She hadn't expected Steve to drop everything and return home after her call, but it appeared he had. To argue with her further? Or to try to charm her into continuing to help him? He wouldn't succeed at either, she vowed.

He tapped sharply on the door. Too impatient to use his keys? Or had he not wanted to startle her? With Annie in her left arm, she threw open the door. "I wasn't expecting you yet, but since you're..."

Her voice faded when she realized the man on the other side of the door was not Steve.

He was fairly young, no older than thirty. Sandy hair. Gray eyes. Heavy chin. Sulky mouth. He eyed her, then glanced at the baby before speaking. "Where is she? Where's Janice?"

Casey frowned as she suddenly realized who this must be. "Janice isn't here. I don't know where she is."

"Don't give me that. You've been helping her. She's hiding here, isn't she?"

"No. I told you she isn't here. Now if you'll excuse me, I—"

He reached out to shove the door open when she would have closed it in his face. "I know she's here, damn it. I want to talk to her."

His raised voice startled the baby, who began to fuss. Casey instinctively turned her attention to Annie for a moment. By the time she looked up, the man she assumed was Janice's abusive lover, Rick Walls, was inside the house. "What the...? Get out of here!"

Ignoring her, he moved swiftly toward the bedrooms. "Janice?"

"I told you, she's *not here*. Now if you don't get out, I'll..."

She might as well have been talking to the rocking chair. Walls moved from room to room, opening doors, searching grimly for Janice. Only after he'd checked the last room—the kitchen—did he seem to concede that Casey had been telling the truth. "Where is she?"

"What part of 'I don't know' do you not understand?"

Her insolent answer made his eyes narrow and spark with anger. "You expect me to believe that?"

"I don't care what you believe. She isn't here, and I don't know where she is. To be honest, I wouldn't tell you if I did know. Now, please leave."

"Fine. I'll take my kid and get out. You tell Janice if she wants the kid, she'll have to come to me."

Casey's arms tightened protectively around the baby. "You aren't touching this baby."

His jaw hardened. "I don't see how you can stop me."

"But I will," she answered flatly. "I'm responsible for this child and I'm not letting her out of my sight." Walls hadn't even seemed in the least interested in the baby until now, when he had decided he could use her as leverage against Janice. Casey had no intention of allowing him to do that, no matter what it took to stop him.

Her defiance seemed to enrage him. "Maybe you want to call the police? Maybe you want to explain to them why you think you've got a right to keep a kid from its own father after the mother ran out on it? You think they're going to let you—a stranger—keep her? Or that Lockhart guy, who's got no more business butting into my affairs than you do?"

For a moment the threat shook her. Casey knew full well that her custody of Annie was on shaky ground, that the authorities would insist she should have called them immediately. She could all too easily picture Annie being taken away by stern-faced strangers, herself being led out in handcuffs by uniformed police officers. But then she regained control of her runaway imagination and brought herself back to reality.

She shook her head. "You don't really want to call

the police. I happen to know there's a restraining order against you. You aren't supposed to go anywhere near Janice. And you are not coming close to this baby."

"We'll see about that," he said, taking a step toward her.

Casey backed away, her heart pounding against her chest. She could make a run for it, she thought swiftly. The front door was still standing open behind her. If she held Annie very snugly and ran as fast as she could, there was a chance she could get away. Once she got out in the street, she would scream until someone came to her aid.

The first priority was protecting the baby.

"Give me the kid," Walls demanded.

Casey whirled to run.

She might have made it had her long hair not swung out behind her with the movement. She'd taken only a couple of steps when she was jerked back so sharply and painfully that it brought tears to her eyes and made her involuntarily cry out. Already distressed, Annie began to wail noisily.

His hand still fisted in Casey's hair, Walls yanked her backward. "I said, give me the kid," he repeated loudly. "Now, damn it!"

"No!" Casey kicked out at him, now as furious, if not more so, than he was. "Get your hands off me, you—"

He lifted his free hand, apparently intent on hitting her. She braced for an impact that never came.

There was a blur of movement from somewhere behind her and then Walls was suddenly flying across the room. He landed with a loud crash and a jarring thud against a wall behind him.

"You want a fight?" Steve said, looming over the intruder in his house with murder in his eyes. "You just got yourself one. Get up, Walls. Let's see how you stand up against someone closer to your own size."

Rocking the screaming baby comfortingly in her arms, Casey felt her shoulders sag. "It's all right, sweetie. Everything's okay now," she murmured, pressing her lips to Annie's silky forehead. "Steve's here."

Maybe she was still furious with him. And maybe she didn't trust him farther than she could throw him, when it came to business. But if there was one thing Casey did believe, it was that Steve would never let any harm come to this baby, or to her.

He would give his life for them, if it came to that—and she assured herself fervently that it wouldn't.

In that respect, at least, she trusted him completely.

12

STEVE HAD NEVER thought of himself as a violent man. Rarely in his adult life had he had the impulse to do bodily harm to anyone. And he'd certainly never felt even the slightest urge to kill.

That had changed the moment he'd walked into his house and had seen this bastard's fist in Casey's hair, his other hand poised to strike her. Just the realization that Casey and Annie were being threatened had made fury erupt in Steve like a volcano. He didn't even clearly remember hitting the guy, he thought as he leaned over him.

He would make sure to remember the next time he hit him. "Get up," he repeated softly.

"Steve..." Casey murmured from behind him.

"Take the baby and go somewhere safe, Casey. Her carrier is beside the couch."

"No, I..."

"No!" Walls struggled to his feet, wiping a trickle of blood from the corner of his mouth with the back of one hand. "That's my kid. You got no right to take her anywhere."

"First, you have no proof that this is your child. For all you know, she could be mine. But regardless of that, we're taking care of her now, and you aren't touching her."

Walls made a move toward Steve, but backed off when Steve spread his feet and held up his hands in a beckoning manner. "Just try it," he challenged.

For only a moment, Walls looked tempted. Steve almost hoped the other guy would give him an excuse to pound his face in. But then Walls dropped his fists.

"Wise move, my man," someone said from the still-open doorway, the words just audible over the baby's cries.

Steve glanced over his shoulder. Looking perfectly at ease amid the chaos in the living room, Blake leaned against the doorjamb. Steve knew his almost lazy pose was deceptive; should Steve need assistance getting Wells out of his house, there was no one he'd have preferred at his side more than Blake.

"Who the hell are you?" Walls demanded.

"Just call me Blake. I'm a private investigator, and I know a great deal more about you than you can probably imagine, Walls. I think you'd better go before I put some of it to good use."

Outnumbered now, Walls ground his teeth. "All right, I'll go. But you can tell Janice I'll be back."

"No, I don't think I will tell her that," Blake said meditatively. "You're facing parole violation charges, Walls. Several of them, I believe. Ignoring the restraining order Janice has against you isn't going to sit well with the authorities. I've talked to Janice and we're working out a plan to make sure you never get near her or the baby again. I'd advise you to put her behind you and get on with your life—such as it is."

"Don't tell me what to do," Walls snapped, almost trembling with impotent frustration.

Blake shrugged. "It was just a suggestion. By the way, I've got quite a few friends in the Missouri legal system. A couple of calls from me and you'll be back behind bars in a matter of days. Since I don't think you want that, I'd suggest you get lost."

"I've got a few friends in local law enforcement," Steve added. "They won't care much for the way you broke into my house and assaulted my friend."

Confident now that Walls was subdued, Steve stepped close to Casey and ran a hand over the hair Walls had yanked so viciously. "Are you all right?" he asked her.

She nodded, patting Annie's back. "Just get him out of here."

"With pleasure." Steve looked at the other man and motioned toward the door. "Get out. And stay away from Janice, her baby, and Casey, or you'll have me to deal with."

"And me," Blake added.

"Ms. Gibson's family would probably like me to add their names to that list," Frank Claybrook commented as he entered the house. "She has a couple of brothers who didn't take kindly to finding out their little sister had unwittingly become involved with an abuser. There were some vague threats about breaking bones and bashing teeth—I don't think I'd mess with them, if I were you, Walls."

Steve wondered how many more people were going to wander uninvited into his house. Maybe he should close the front door—after he'd booted Walls through it, of course.

Walls tried one last attempt at bravado. "You can't keep me from my kid."

"The courts can," Steve said. "I suggest you hire a lawyer if you really want to fight for visitation rights. I hope you can afford the best—that's what it's going to take for you to ever set eyes on this little girl again."

Growling obscenities, Walls stormed out. Blake reached out and closed the door.

"Well," he said. "That was pleasant."

Casey rolled her eyes and shifted Annie to her shoulder. The baby had stopped crying now and was beginning to suck her fingers, something that seemed to have become a soothing habit for her. "Were you serious?" she asked Steve. "About Walls getting an attorney, I mean? Is there a chance that he could get custody of Annie?"

Blake was the one who answered. "Not a chance in hell. You haven't seen Walls's record. I have. No sane judge would trust him with an infant."

Casey looked at him. "Have you really talked to Janice? Do you know where she is?"

In answer, Blake walked to the door that led into

the kitchen. "He's gone now, Janice. Why don't you join us?"

Steve watched Casey's jaw drop when Janice walked into the room. He imagined he wore much the same stunned look.

"Janice," he said, stepping quickly forward to greet the heartbreakingly pale and fragile-looking young woman. "Are you okay?"

She looked at him through the tears that swam in her dark eyes. "I'm so sorry to have gotten you involved with this. I didn't know where else to turn. I didn't know what else to do when that man found me in the hospital and told me I had to take Annie and go back to Rick. I panicked. I was so afraid Rick would hurt Annie. I thought if I could leave her someplace safe and lead him away from her, maybe I could come back afterward and take her away with me where he couldn't find us. I guess—I guess I didn't think it out very well. I was so scared."

Steve reached out to rest a supportive hand on her shoulder. He could almost feel her bones through the thin fabric of her shirt. She looked as though she could keel over any minute. "Why don't you sit down in the rocking chair with your baby?" he suggested gently. "I'll get everyone some coffee and we can talk."

He watched as Casey approached Janice with a smile. "It's so good to see you, Janice. I know Annie has missed you," she told her, her voice warm.

Janice returned the smile shyly. "Mr.—um, Blake

told me how much you've been helping with her. I don't know how to thank you, Ms. Jansen."

"You can start by calling me Casey. And taking care of this beautiful baby was no hardship at all. I feel as though I should thank you for allowing me to spend time with her."

If Steve hadn't already been head over heels in love with Casey, he would have fallen at that moment. She was being so kind to Janice, so sympathetic. Granted, Janice had made some bad choices, but now was not the time to remind her of them. Now she needed friends—and she had them here.

Janice wiped her hands on the oversized T-shirt she wore. "I'm a little nervous about taking her," she admitted to Casey. "I'm sure she doesn't even remember me. She'll probably think I'm a stranger."

"Nonsense. You've only been gone a few days. She'll know her mommy. Why don't you sit down and I'll lay her in your arms? I think that will be the easiest way to make the transfer."

Janice followed Casey's suggestion and a moment later, Annie was in her arms, staring up at her in rather fierce concentration. "See?" Casey said with a smile. "She knows exactly who you are."

She took a step backward. "She's probably going to be hungry soon. I'll go make a bottle for her."

Janice didn't even seem to hear her as she bent over her baby, making adoring sounds to her.

Steve turned to Blake when Casey left the room. "Want to catch me up here?"

Blake had been talking quietly to Claybrook. They both turned to Steve.

"Janice had decided to return to her family in St. Louis," Blake explained. "They've sent a message through Frank, here, that they want her to come home. They want to meet Annie, and they want to help them get on their feet."

"My parents sent a letter," Janice added. "They asked me to forgive them for everything they did to hurt me, and they've forgiven me for the things I did to hurt them. They promised to treat me like an adult if I come home, and to put the past behind us. I think it will be good for me and for Annie to go back. Annie needs to know her grandparents and her uncles and cousins."

"Yes," Steve agreed with a smile. "She does. As much as we'll miss you here, I think you've made the right decision, Janice."

She nodded. "They've promised to assist me in the situation with Rick, too. One of my brothers is a St. Louis cop. He sent word that he can help me."

"Good." Steve knew how hard it was for a woman to get away from an abusive man. Too many had died trying. But perhaps Walls would think twice about bothering Janice now that she wasn't alone and vulnerable to him.

He wondered if there was anything he could do to make certain of that.

Casey returned with the bottle. "I heard everything from the kitchen," she confessed. "I'm glad you're going back to your family, Janice. I hope everything works out for you."

"Thank you, Ms.—um, Casey."

Claybrook was set to accompany Janice back to her family. He was driving a rental car, he explained. They would fly back as soon as they could make arrangements.

"That's not a problem," Steve said. "I'll call B.J., my pilot. He'll take you this afternoon."

"You can use one of my planes," Casey asserted quickly. "I'm sure there's one ready to fly right now...and a pilot to take you."

Blake chuckled. "It's not often you have rival companies both offering free flights," he said to Janice. "You'd better take advantage of it while you can."

"I won't choose between you," she said with a faint smile. "I'm sure whatever the two of you work out will be fine."

Claybrook nodded. "A free charter flight sounds good to me. Let me know when and where and I'll make arrangements with Janice's family."

Casey looked at Steve with a renewed hint of resentment in her eyes. "You offered first," she muttered. "If B.J. isn't available, let me know and I'll call one of my pilots."

He nodded. He hadn't meant to irritate her again. Seemed like just about anything he did had that effect today.

He was ready to speed his guests on their way so

he could try to repair his budding relationship with Casey. "I'll call B.J."

Casey nodded. "I'll get Annie's things together. We bought her a few necessities," she added to Janice.

"Thank you. I'd like to repay you..."

"You'll do no such thing. Consider it a parting gift from your employers."

Janice's eyes filled with tears again. "Thank you." She looked from Casey to Steve. "Thank you both. Annie and I owe you so much."

Both Casey and Steve muttered something appropriate and hurried away, uncomfortable with Janice's expression of gratitude.

IT WAS surprisingly difficult for Casey to say goodbye to Annie. She'd known the baby only a couple of days, she reminded herself.

But she was going to miss her.

"Be a good girl for Mommy, Annie," she murmured, pressing a kiss on the baby's forehead.

Steve then stepped forward to claim his own baby kiss. "Let her get some sleep tonight, will you, kid? She looks as if she could use it."

Carrying Annie's things, Claybrook escorted Janice out. As the door closed behind them, Casey ran a hand through her hair, a bit disoriented that everything had ended so quickly. Only a few hours earlier, they hadn't even known where Janice was, and now she'd shown up, reclaimed her baby and left again.

Janice could have no way of knowing, of course, that her choices this weekend had changed Casey's life so very drastically.

Steve had turned to Blake. "Thanks, Blake. I really appreciate everything you did. I don't know how you found Janice, and I doubt that you'd tell me if I asked, but I want you to know..."

Blake cut in abruptly, as uncomfortable with the gratitude as Casey and Steve had been earlier. "Forget it, Steve. I owed you a hell of a lot more than this. You saved my life in Mexico."

Casey blinked. "You saved his life?" she asked Steve, having no idea the "favor" they'd alluded to had been so momentous.

Steve looked embarrassed. "He's exaggerating."

"Not at all," Blake murmured. "Nevertheless, a couple of days work is hardly adequate repayment. Any time you need me again, feel free to call."

Steve shook his friend's hand. "Same goes. Give my regards to your wife, Blake. And good luck with that new baby."

"Thanks." Blake glanced quickly at Casey before looking at Steve again. "Good luck to you, too."

"Thanks." Steve, too, cast a quick glance at Casey as he spoke.

She glared at him in return. As kind as he'd been to Janice, she hadn't forgotten how he'd stabbed *her* in the back earlier.

Blake took Casey's hand, then leaned over to kiss her cheek. "It's been a pleasure meeting you, ma'am," he murmured in a humorous drawl. "Give my buddy a break, okay?"

"I might just give him several breaks," she muttered in return, making Blake laugh.

"Looks like you've got a real challenge ahead for you now, my friend," he said to Steve on the way out.

Casey watched as Steve's smile flashed a bit dangerously. "I'm aware of that. But I'm ready."

Casey waited only until Blake was gone before reaching for her purse. "Now that everything is settled, I have to go. I still have time to run by my office for an hour or two this afternoon."

"We have to talk."

"There's nothing to say," she insisted, avoiding his eyes. "Janice and Annie are safe, you and I can feel good about having done a good deed, and now it's over. We can go back to the way things were before—me running my business, you doing everything you can to undermine my efforts."

"Casey, I didn't steal Jack Alexander away from you."

"Oh?" She lifted an eyebrow in disbelief. "So he *didn't* sign a contract with you?"

"Well, yes, but—"

She nodded. "That's what I thought."

She moved toward the exit.

Steve placed a hand on the door to keep her from opening it. "Jack Alexander came to me two weeks ago," he said flatly. "He asked me to work him up a bid for regular air charter service. I did so. I had no way of knowing you had given him the idea or that you'd been actively pursuing his business. Nor did I have any way of knowing what terms you offered him. I assumed he would ask you for a bid, too, but that's only smart business sense. I made him a good offer, and he accepted it. That was all there was to it."

"Fine. I wish you well with him. Now, will you please move out of the way so I can go?"

"No. We're going to talk about this. Why are you so angry with me? Do you honestly want me to turn away potential customers who come to me just to give you a break? Is that really the way you want this to go, Casey?"

She scowled, feeling trapped by his words. "I don't know what I want you to do. I only know that we can't make this work between you and me. How can we try to destroy each other during the day and be..."

"Lovers," he supplied for her when she faltered.

"...lovers," she repeated through clenched teeth, finishing the question, "after hours?"

"I think we can find a way. It's going to take some creative thinking, of course, a few compromises, but there's no reason we can't work something out that would be beneficial to both of us. There really is room for two charter services in this area, Casey. We can find a way to handle this."

She shook her head. "I can't," she answered simply. "Every time I lose a customer to you, I would feel betrayed. Maybe that isn't professional and mature, but I can't help it. I can't see you as both a lover and a rival."

"Then how about just a lover?" Steve said quietly.

Her frown deepened. "I don't know what you mean."

"How would you like to buy a couple of planes for your company at a good price? And of course you'll need a couple more pilots to fly them for you. I know two who would be available. B.J., and myself. And I'd like you to try to find a position for Madelyn. She'll earn her salary, believe me."

She blinked a couple of times, then shook her head. "I'm not buying this. You're just trying to make a grand gesture to prove a point or something. Well, it won't work, Steve. I—"

"I am completely serious," he said, his expression utterly sincere. "If Lockhart Air is an unsurmountable obstacle between us, then we have to remove it. You're more important to me than my name on a shingle."

She reached out blindly to lay a land on the nearest wall, stunned by his offer. By the realization that he really was serious. "Have you lost your mind?"

"No," he answered simply. "I've lost my heart."

Her own heart pounding frantically, she shook her head again. "No. You don't mean it. You love that company. It's been your dream. Your passion. It's everything to you. You said so yourself."

"I love *you*. You are my dream. My passion. You mean everything to me. The business is just a job—admittedly, one that I've enjoyed, but as long as I can fly, and as long as I can be with you, I'll be happy."

She couldn't seem to stop shaking her head. Panic had gripped her, and seemed to be squeezing her throat. It was very difficult for her to speak. "You can't—you don't—you aren't—"

His smile was crooked. "<u>All</u> of the above. I can. I do. And I am. I love you, Casey."

"Oh, my God."

"I'll give you a little time to think about it before you give me an answer, of course. You think half an hour will be long enough?"

"Don't—"

"Okay, an hour. I really don't think I can wait any longer than that. I've been waiting so long already."

Her head was spinning. She put her free hand to her temple. "You really think you've been in...in love with me for months?"

"I don't think it. I know it. And so do B.J. and Madelyn. They've ribbed me about it mercilessly."

"Steve, you hardly even know me."

"I know you better than you know yourself, I think," he replied, his voice so warm and tender that it brought a new lump to her already tight throat. "And you're everything I've ever wanted. Every time I saw you holding Annie this weekend, all I could think about was how much I wished she was our baby. I don't know how you feel about kids, but

I'm crazy about them. You don't have a problem with being my boss *and* my wife, do you?"

"Oh, God." This was getting worse and worse. She felt as though her whole body was going weak. "You said you couldn't work for someone like me."

"I'll learn. And so will B.J. Although I can't guarantee he's going to like those neat little khaki shirts you make your pilots wear. They really aren't his style, you know. But you can discuss that with him."

Casey was appalled to realize that tears were trickling down her cheeks. Steve had just offered to give up the business he loved so deeply. For her. So she could continue to run the business that had always been her father's dream, and never her own.

She shook her head. "I can't do it. I can't let you give up Lockhart Air. You'd hate me."

"Never."

"I don't care what you say now, it won't work. I won't do it."

"Then would you consider a partnership?" he suggested instead, seeming to take encouragement from something he saw in her eyes. "We make a good team, you know. Look at how well we handled this weird weekend. You're a whiz with numbers and business forecasts and organization. I've been known to be pretty good with planes and people. Between the two of us, we could probably figure out a way to put both our talents to work for one big company, don't you think? Jansen-Lockhart Charter Services. Partners. Fifty-fifty."

Jansen-Lockhart. There was a certain ring to it, she thought dazedly. And her father's name still came first. "Maybe it could work."

"You bet it could." He reached out to skim his knuckles over her cheek, leaving a trail of tingles behind. "Give us a chance, Casey, darlin'. I'll make sure you aren't sorry."

A fresh wave of tears followed the first. "I didn't want to fall in love with you."

"I know you didn't. It was downright mean of me to make you, wasn't it?"

"I didn't trust you."

"No. But you should have. I've never done anything to purposefully hurt you. I never will."

"I was afraid of you."

He wiped a tear away from her cheek with his thumb. "I know you were, darlin'. And you terrified me from the time I first saw you and felt my heart fall on the ground at your feet. I guess that's just part of this falling in love thing."

"Maybe it is," she whispered.

His mouth hovered an inch above hers. "Casey?"

"I love you, Steve. I still don't know if it makes sense, but I love you. I guess...I guess I have for as long as I've known you. Why else would I have fought it so hard?"

He was smiling when he kissed her. But the smile quickly faded into fervent need. She locked her arms around his neck and returned an embrace that nearly overwhelmed her.

Steve did everything with passion, she mused, knowing that was part of what had drawn her to him.

He was everything she wasn't. Everything she wanted, she thought.

And now he could be hers, with only a word from her.

He lifted her head. "Well?"

She paused only long enough to make him worry a little. He deserved that, she thought, considering how many times he'd done the same to her. And then she smiled. "Yes," she said simply.

His hug nearly crushed her ribcage. For once, she didn't complain.

"ABOUT THOSE KHAKI SHIRTS," Steve murmured, hours later.

She smiled and ran a hand over his bare chest as she lay nude and exhausted against him. "What about them?"

"I really don't think we're going to get B.J. into them."

"Maybe if he tried it, he'd like it."

"Don't count on it."

She gave an exaggerated sigh. "Oh, well. I suppose we can make a few exceptions."

"You aren't going to insist that I wear one, are you?"

Chuckling, she walked her fingers down his chest to his belly button. "I don't know. I think they're kind of sexy. I think I'd really enjoy taking them off you."

He groaned. "Maybe I wouldn't mind wearing khaki, after all. As long as I get to choose your clothes, of course."

Picturing fishnet and Lycra, Casey laughed and shook her head. "I don't think so."

"Well, it was worth a shot," he said, capturing her hand as it wandered into dangerous territory. He lifted it to his lips and placed a kiss in her palm. "This is going to be a very interesting relationship, you know."

"I know." She still couldn't believe it was real. But she was getting there.

"Casey?"

"Hmm?" She was concentrating on how good it felt to nuzzle his throat and feel his pulse against her cheek.

"How do you think your father would feel about this?"

She went still for a moment, then shrugged. "I think he would approve. He always rather admired you, you know. He wouldn't have been so worried about you if he hadn't thought you were good at what you did."

"So you're okay with it? You've put all that to rest?"

She lifted her head to look at him. "I loved my father. I spent my whole life trying to please him. Sometimes I succeeded, sometimes I didn't. But he's gone now, and it's time I start pleasing myself. That means making my own choices—following my own dreams—for the first time in my life. Maybe I'll enjoy running the business end of Jansen-Lockhart Charter Service. Maybe I'll want to hand it all over to you and do something else eventually. I don't know. But whatever I decide, it'll be for my sake, not for my father's."

"Whatever you decide, I'll be there beside you, cheering you on," Steve told her, approval written on his face. "I have every faith that you can do anything you want to do."

"Oh, really. Well, the first thing I want to do..." She leaned over to whisper something into his ear.

Steve's laugh was a bit rough-edged. "I will definitely cheer you on," he assured her. "I'm ready when you are, Casey, darlin'. Let's fly."

Laughing with him, she opened her arms to him in preparation for takeoff.

She believed her longtime fear of flying was well on the way to being conquered for good.

If you enjoyed what you just read,
then we've got an offer you can't resist!

Take 2 bestselling love stories FREE!

Plus get a FREE surprise gift!

HARLEQUIN®
Makes any time special ™

WIN A DREAM

In celebration of Harlequin®'s golden anniversary

Enter to win a *dream!* You could win:

- A luxurious trip for two to *The Renaissance Cottonwoods Resort* in Scottsdale, Arizona, or
- A bouquet of flowers once a week for a year from **FTD**, or
- A $500 shopping spree, or
- A fabulous bath & body gift basket, including **K-tel**'s *Candlelight and Romance* 5-CD set.

Look for **WIN A DREAM** flash on specially marked Harlequin® titles by Penny Jordan, Dallas Schulze, Anne Stuart and Kristine Rolofson in October 1999*.

FTD

RENAISSANCE. COTTONWOODS RESORT
SCOTTSDALE, ARIZONA

K·TEL

*No purchase necessary—for contest details send a self-addressed envelope to Harlequin Makes Any Time Special Contest, P.O. Box 9069, Buffalo, NY, 14269-9069 (include contest name on self-addressed envelope). Contest ends December 31, 1999. Open to U.S. and Canadian residents who are 18 or over. Void where prohibited.

PHMATS-GR